Bound to the Wild

Jasmine Heighway

Contents

Prologue

M ates:

Both female and male wolves can identify whom their mate is starting when they turn 18, no matter the age of their mate. It is easier for male wolves to find their mate because their senses are sharper than she wolves.

Each wolf will gain his or her own individual scent upon turning of age. All werewolves that belong to a pack that are under the age of 18 don't have their own distinct scent – they only carry their common pack scent, which can be easily identifiable by any wolf.

Most male wolves find their mate either right after they turn 18, or within the next two years – it is how fate works. Because of this, most couples tend to have children really young. Just like regular wolves, males are the dominant sex among their kind and are almost always the gender in charge, but that doesn't mean the females have absolutely no say at all. Some things have evolved amongst their kind through the years, but not much. Most female werewolves refuse to leave their pups alone once they're born and choose to stay at home with them and take care of them. It is in a she wolf's

DNA to want to bear pups for her mate, as well as protecting them with her life.

After the first two years of turning 18 passes, the chance of a male/female finding their mate becomes really slim. It is rare that a wolf over the age of 22 ever finds their mate if they haven't already. Older wolves that don't find their mates end up surrendering to their wolf side and life out the rest of their life as a rogue until they die and are finally connected with their other half.

A mate is THE single most important thing to a werewolf, besides the pups that they will have together. It is very common for a male werewolf to be possessive and borderline obsessive over their mate - but it's multiplied ten fold for alphas, because they are naturally more primal than the average werewolf. A male wolf will always want to be around his mate, and if separated from their mate for too long of a time period, they can go crazy. Constant touching is common amongst mated pairs. A male wolf will do anything to keep their mate happy; it is their main priority.

Alphas, Betas, and Gammas

Most high-ranking wolves retire from their position and pass it down to their first born once they turn 25. This will give the next generation of leaders a chance to find their mate, and start their family before needing to focus on taking care of the pack, as well giving them enough time to fully mature.

Ideally, the main leading positions are passed down to males. The high-ranking females are in charge of being the pack nurturers.

Mate's Ball

In order to assist wolves in finding their other half who may live in another pack, there is an annual ball held during the winter by the werewolf council. All wolves that are of age, or those who have not found their mate already, attend the ball, which takes place after the first week of the New Year.

Every Alpha and Luna from the U.S. must attend; as well as bringing all of their pack's unmated she and he wolves. If you don't find your mate there, it is up to the individual wolf to travel around the world and find their mate on their own. Because of the large number of werewolves that attend the event every year, they host the ball on a private island owned by the council. Most wolves will find their mates at the ball.

Chapter 1

"Alright, now we're going to move on to everyone's favorite topic besides mating. Female maturation." Our teacher paused to avoid having to talk over the hoops and hollers of all the douchey unmated males in the class. Rolling my eyes, I crossed my arms over my chest - not even making an attempt to conceal my annoyance as our teacher tried, and failed, to quiet the class down.

Moments like these were the only times I was actually thankful for being a weak little Omega. When it came to mating and bearing pups, most males wolves everywhere only ever sought after strong, high-ranking she wolves. It was in our basic nature to want a strong lineage. It was in a male wolf's DNA to be automatically attracted to a female with large, wide hips because those females typically carried the strongest heirs. Just like it was in a female wolf's DNA to seek after power and strength, because they were the best protectors and could adequately protect a family.

But, with that being said, when it came to meaningless flirting and quick fucks, I was always the desired target. Well, me along with every other Omega female in my pack. Omegas were usually never paired with a high-ranking pack member, so males usually didn't care about upsetting someone's future mate by taking their other half's virtue. It was hard keeping the wandering hands off my body at all times, as well as making sure I didn't ever put myself in a position to be cornered by one or more shit head wolves who thought it was okay to take something that someone wasn't willing to give them, but I had managed over the last 17 years.

I had endured so many crude remarks and comments from any and every higher-ranking unmated male in my pack, that I'd honestly lost count at this point. It was never ending – mainly because I couldn't fight back – even if I so desperately wanted to. I usually got the worst of the crude remarks and disrespectful ass smacks. This was all due to the fact that, not to be vain, I was one of the prettier she wolves we had in our pack. Not to mention, the least annoying and demanding.

You weren't allowed to ask for things as an Omega. You simply took what you were given and never complained. You only ever spoke up if you wanted a good smacking. At least, that's how our pack was run. I've heard stories from girls that have been transferred to our pack after the Mate's Ball about other packs actually respecting and treating their lower ranking members like actual human beings - but that was just hear say mumble jumble that you could never quite trust.

"Alright, ALRIGHT! Enough. So, I'm going to go ahead and preface this lesson with some basic info about mating, which you all should know since we just covered that unit last week. As you all know, a male wolf can detect his mate after he's turned 18, no matter the age of his other half, whereas a female's mate must be of legal age for her to be able to sense the bond pre-marking. Now, maturation for every female were will take place on the day of her 18th birthday. This is why we refer to 18 as the "legal age". It really has nothing to do with males at all, the only change they go through is acquiring their own personal scent. Mark that down in your notes; it will be a question on your test later next week." Our teacher paused as the sound of pencils scraping across paper filled the room.

"Continuing on, a female's wolf will recognize the need to adapt its human side in order to attract her mate and also be in prime shape to bear the strongest pups she can possibly produce. A female will know exactly at what moment her body is sent into maturation, as it is said to be remarkably painful. I can tell you all from experience that that part is very much true." A few girls started whining while guys high-fived each other about the joys of "having a dick". From the way some of them acted, I knew they had more dick in their personality than in their pants.

"Now, maturation brings about a couple distinct changes to a female's body. First, just like male wolves, she will finally obtain her own scent - which will replace the common pack scent that all underage pack wolves carry. Secondly, her hips and breast will enlarge, both of which vary from female to female. The size of the female's hips is an indicator of her mate's ranking and the strength of their future pups."

"Lastly, she might have a few other unnecessary physical changes. These can include..." I completely zoned out, having heard the important parts that would most likely be on the test. I was almost asleep, so beautifully close I could almost taste it – until I felt something light hit the back of my head. I jerked my head up and searched the room for the culprit when my eyes fell upon the two biggest assholes in my grade. Kyler and Miller, the Alpha's nephews. They were trying to contain their laughter as they pointed to the piece of paper that had bounced off my head and landed at my feet. I clenched my teeth to keep myself from lashing out at them before leaning over and grabbing the crumpled up note.

When you want to become a real woman, you know where we'll be. After all, an Omega's mate can never satisfy with such a tiny dick.

My chest rose and fell rapidly as my anger spiked to a new high I've never reached before. How dare they insinuate that simply because I'm a low ranking, my mate will be so weak that they won't be able to satisfy me. Bile quickly rose in my throat at how disgusting those two boys truly were. Vile. They're both absolutely vile.

My wolf began pressing against our mental barrier, begging me to let her out so she could make sure they were never able to recreate humans as awful as themselves. I agreed they needed to be removed from the gene pool, and there's no one that wants to do it more than I, but that was a death wish waiting to happen.

The amount of sheer effort it took to hold her back was physically, and mentally, exhausting. My head began to throb with the promise of a migraine. Thankfully, the bell rang not but a second later. I snatched my books off my desk in a death grip before bolting for the door. I decided it would be in my best interest to skip my next period and try making an attempt to calm my wolf before I did something I would seriously regret. Pulling my phone from my bra (here's a secret Victoria, give us a fucking pocket for our leggings) I typed out a quick text to one of my best-friends, Leighton, informing him that if his cousins suddenly came up missing, I needed him to be my alibi.

So rough day I take it then? He replied a few seconds later.

You have no fucking idea. We still on for that Harry Potter marathon?

Wouldn't miss it for the world. Dad is out checking on the training facilities in the north sector for the rest of the night. I'll just pick you up from school.

Content that I would have an adequate distraction from my shitty life problems after school, I strode to my favorite secluded hallway and slumped against the wall, pulling out my homework that I failed to do last night to pass time before lunch rolled around.

I made my way towards the cafeteria, trying to calm my nerves that were building with every step. This was a daily routine for all Omegas. Lunchtime - or torture time as I liked to call it - was the worst. If I had a dollar for every time someone slapped my ass or copped a feel of my boobs while I was waiting for my food, I would be the next Warren Buffett. But, days like today were always especially bad because my only other friend besides Leighton, Mickie, was gone for a training evaluation.

All children who's parents were pack warriors were test-ed once a month after they turned 16 to make sure they were keeping up their technique and meeting the pack's fighting standards. I always thought the whole thing was a little extreme. There were rumors that still lingered about what pack life was like almost two decades ago. We were more relaxed and carefree back then, but then our southern ally, the Bloodlust pack, turned against us and ever since we've been on constant edge. Always training rigorously and making sure security was at its max.

I maneuvered my way through the lunchroom without a single incident so far, which is a good sign. I was almost in the clear with my peanut butter and jelly sandwich and water in hand when I was suddenly stopped about ten feet from the cafeteria double doors.

"Are you sure you should be eating that many carbs, Aceso? I mean, you're starting to get saddlebags. We wouldn't want your mate to have any reason to reject you, would we? Besides, being an Omega is shitty enough as it is." I bit the inside of my cheek so hard I drew blood, but - try as I might - I couldn't keep the snarky comment on the tip of my tongue from slipping through my lips.

"Well, Savannah, we don't all have daddies who can give us free nose jobs and liposuction whenever we please, like you, now do we? By the way, did your new lip injections hurt?" I posed the question as innocent as possible, but by the scrunched up look on her face, I knew I hit a tender nerve. I'm so going to get my ass kicked.

She shot her hand up to grab my neck with her bony hands, but I was faster than her. I quickly dodged her death claws and ducked under her arm, sprinting the rest of the way towards the safety of the library. That bitch wouldn't step foot in here. It's as if she thinks knowledge will magically turn her ugly.

Too late I snickered to myself under my breath.

By the time classes were finally over, I was ready to rip someone's head off. Climbing into Leighton's sleek Aston Martin, I slammed the door harder than need be and threw my head back against its rest while letting out a deep sigh.

"Sounds like someone's shitty day got even worse?" Leighton questioned.

"Oh, you know. The usual; Savannah being a total bitch just because she can be and some random dude reaching up my skirt while I was bent over trying to get a drink from the water fountain. No big fucking deal." I growled out.

"Being the pack doctor's daughter does have its advantages I guess. And you do have a great ass. It's hard to not want to touch." He replied while shrugging his shoulders, making a horrible attempt at cheering me up.

"Shut up asshole, you aren't helping." I muttered and shot him my best side glare. He returned it with a wounded look and placed his hand over his heart.

"Wow, Cece, that one really hurt. Right here." He said, tapping the place where his heart would be.

"Yeah, yeah, yeah. Just drive. I've got a Kit Kat in my kitchen that's screaming my name and some wizard shit to watch. Let's get a move on." I said, clapping my hands in an impatient manner. He hesitated a second before returning his attention to the road and pulling into traffic. The action caught me off guard because it was something Leighton never did; he was always sure of himself.

"Alright, what's the matter? Spill." I demanded. He let out the breath he'd been holding and skittishly glanced my way before focusing his gaze back on the road.

"It's about the Mate's Ball." He said, clearing his throat before audibly swallowing.

"And...?" I pressed him, moving my hand in a circle motion. I was trying my best to be patient with him, but it really wasn't my strong suit.

"Well, as you know, you turn eighteen the day we leave for the island. That means you'll be required to attend the ball with us. I talked to my father, and convinced him to let me escort you with me. He didn't really understand why, but he didn't put up a fight either. Your parents agreed that it's a good idea, since you can't really protect yourself." My wolf growled loudly in my head, causing me to wince slightly. She absolutely hated it when people undermined our abilities.

"Whatever." I said with finality in my tone, letting him know that I had no intention on participating in this conversation any longer. I could tell by his body language that he was frustrated with my answer, but I honestly didn't give a shit at this point. I loved Leighton like a brother, I really did. He was one of my closest (and only) friends, but sometimes I wish he would just leave me be and let nature run its course.

I settled into my normal chair at the dinner table after seeing Leighton out. I could tell my parents were aware that he'd told me all about their plans to have him escort me to the ball, because they were wary of the attitude I was most likely going to have. I refused to look up and meet their expectant eyes as I ate. The only sound to be heard was that of our forks scraping over our plates. My mom finally decided to be the brave soul to speak first. She cleared her throat to capture my attention, though I still kept my gaze concentrated on my food as if it were the most interesting thing in the world.

"Well, Aceso, I was thinking maybe we could go out tomorrow night after you get home from school and pick out a gown for you to take to the ball. After all, first impressions are everything and this is your mate-"

"I'll probably be busy. You know, school and all." I replied, effectively cutting her off. I knew I was being a bitch, but I just couldn't help it. I was so sick and fucking tired of everybody deciding things for me without even thinking to consult me first.

"Aceso, sweetheart, I know you're upset, but please just know it wasn't our doing this time. It was an Alpha order." She spoke timidly.

"What are you talking about "Alpha order"? Leighton told me he convinced his dad to let him take me. Alpha Jackson doesn't even like him hanging around with me." I said, narrowing my eyes at her from across the table. I took notice to how she squirmed with discomfort at my penetrating stare, but chose to stay silent anyway.

"Whatever. I'm full and I have homework I need to get done." I said before throwing my utensils onto my plate and angrily stomping upstairs. I slammed my door shut behind me for emphasis. Questions began swirling in my head while my anger continued to rise. Somebody was lying to me.

Whether it was my parents, or best friend, I didn't know. Nor did I care. I just wanted to know why.

I let out a loud huff of frustration, throwing my hands in the air before yanking my shoes off of my feet and belly flopped onto my bed.

My parents have to be the one's lying, right? I thought to myself. Leighton's never lied to me in our ten years of friendship. Then again, I would probably take just about anybody's side over my parents' any day. Our relationship, to put it bluntly, sucked major ass. They were always nagging me about everything: grades, staying out too late running, how I should "put myself out there more. Make some new friends!". Just once I want them to sit down and just talk to me.

The strangest part about the whole relationship was that it wasn't just me who strongly disliked my parents - it was my wolf too. She'd always detested my parents ever since I'd "met" her when I was ten years old. The first time I brought this up to Leighton or Mickie, they'd told me that no matter what had happened between them and their parents, their wolves always came around eventually. They said it was because the need to be close to their loved ones was overwhelming.

I couldn't help but think that things could've possibly been different had I had a sibling to vent to. I've wanted a brother or sister since before I could even remember, but every time I brought this up to my parents when I was little, they would always shrug me off and say that I was enough for the two of them.

"You're just so perfect, we didn't see the need to have another." My mother would always say in her annoyingly perky voice. I rolled my eyes at the thought while reaching over and turning off the lamp on my nightstand. Today had been mentally exhausting. The last thing I wanted to think about was homework, let alone the Mate's Ball coming up this Saturday. Unfortunately, with it so close – just a mere four days away – I couldn't seem to think about anything but. I, along with my wolf, can't wait for the day we find our mate. Your mate is the only thing most people ever really thought about, both before and after you found them.

I couldn't help but silently contemplate Kyler and Miller's note in class today. What if I wasn't happy with my mate? It's practically unheard of, but what if that was just because most Omegas were too scared to speak out against the only thing that could potentially make them happy? We didn't get much in life because of how low our status was, so our mate was the one thing we had to look forward to.

I forced the negative thoughts away as I rolled on my side, gazing at the hypnotically large moon in the sky through the shades covering my window. I closed my heavy eyelids and let my body pull me under the currents of sleep into the dark oblivion of my dreams.

Chapter 2

Aceso's POV

Searing,

Burning,

Sweltering,

Agonizing.

The pain I awoke to was nothing like anything I'd ever been through in my life ever before. It was enough to temporarily crimple me in bed, unable to do anything but breathe, and even that seemed impossible. The weight on my chest refused to let up. My throat began to close when I opened my mouth to scream out for help. My heart rate shot through the roof as I began to panic, tears pricked my eyes in sheer terror.

Am I fucking dying?

I was finally able to move the slightest bit as the minutes ticked on. I began thrashing my body all over my twin size bed while gripping my sheets. I said a silent prayer to not only God, but also the Moon Goddess, to just kill me already and put me out of my misery.

A tingling, numbing sensation started to encompass my entire being beginning in my toes, slowly crawling up my legs, then to my abdomen, and finally engulfing the rest of my body in one final jolt. The weight that was once restricting my chest was released and I shot up in bed. My chest rose and fell rapidly as I took in as much air as possible for my now oxygen-deprived lungs.

My head felt far too heavy for my body at the moment, and my familiar beige room began to spin. I pinched my eyes shut while bunching my unusually long blonde locks in a death grip. I tugged harshly at my scalp, willing the dizziness to go away so I could just think for a second. I tried desperately to keep the bile from rising in my throat, but the wave of nausea that racked my stomach was too much for me to handle after the episode I just experienced.

Did I just go through...? I cut my thoughts short. There was absolutely no way in hell I just went through maturation. It was physically impossible for a female werewolf to mature before her eighteenth birthday. Hell, my birthday wasn't for another three days! But if it wasn't maturation, then what the ever-living fuck was that?

I leaned my head back against my headboard for what seemed like forever, just waiting for the dizzy spell to pass. I carefully peeped one eye open - not wanting to overwhelm my already exhausted senses - and glanced at the alarm clock on my nightstand. I wasn't exactly sure how long I had ended up laying here for after my oh so lovely wake up call, but it was now just mere minutes before the annoying plastic contraption would be blaring at me to get up.

I grumbled to myself as I rubbed my hands over my face grumpily. I thought about possibly trying to play hooky and get out of going to school, but decided to go against my better judgment and attend anyway.

I stood, instantly reaching out for the headboard of my bed for something to support my weight. My legs were like Jell-O as I wobbled on my unsteady limbs. Creeping into my bathroom, I made sure to be careful not to step on the certain floorboards that I knew were extra creaky. I wanted to ensure my parents stayed asleep; no way did I want to have a full-fledged conversation with either of them right now. I glanced in the mirror and ended up choking on my own spit.

I pounded my fist against the middle of my chest, coughing ferociously to try and clear my throat, but I was still unable to catch my breath for the second time this morning. I stared at my reflection in awe, eyes wide as saucers. The girl looking back at me was most definitely not the same girl I remembered seeing last night while brushing my teeth.

Oh shit.

I wracked my brain yet again for any logical explanation, but the signs were all there. And clear as day, might I add. I trailed my hands over my now flawless and tanned skin. I poked my left boob and instantly grimaced at the pain that ensued.

These are definitely new. I thought to myself. My breasts had grown over two cup sizes throughout the night, making them large and imposing. I was never incredibly endowed in the chest area before today. I remember giving Chris Elliott a bloody nose in the fifth grade for telling me he wouldn't be able to pick me out of a line up of boys because I was so flat chested. That incident ended with me spending three days in the pack cells. Let's just say I never spoke or acted out of turn after that.

Disregarding the awful memory, I moved my attention to my now huge hips; no doubt they were intended for carrying pups in the future. What intrigued me to no end, though, was just how wide they actually were. Normally, when omegas fully matured our hips were noticeably smaller than what mine were right now. It was because our pups would never be as large or as strong as say a beta or alpha's pups would be.

I then realized that the added weight to my head was from my newly thickened and lengthened hair. It was still the same pure blonde - almost white – color it's always been, but now it reached clear down my back to my butt. I couldn't deny this for what it was even if I tried. The signs were all there. The enlarged hips and breasts, subtle body changes like my hair, and my now glowing skin. I even smelled different.

I felt around for my wolf, trying to get a feel for what she thought about the situation. As werewolves, we couldn't verbally communicate with our wolves through words, per se, but we were able to access our wolves mood and make an assumption from there. Almost 99% of the time, my assumptions were correct. I also knew that any information my wolf had to offer me was better than anything anyone else could tell me. No matter what, I always followed my wolf's gut.

After a couple of minutes, I could tell she was in the same boat as I. We were both extremely confused, but also very sure about the culprit of this morning's...festivities being due to our maturation. She was also on edge, making me think that this was something I should keep to myself until I knew anything further about the situation.

I released a puff of air through my lips before cutting off our link and making my way into the shower. I made a conscious effort to avoid letting the water touch my hair. I had planned to wash it this morning, but I had no doubt in my mind that it wouldn't be dry by the time I got to school. Not with the extra mass I now had to deal with.

Once done, I gathered my long waves up into a messy ponytail and threw on one of Leighton's baseball sweatshirts that I'd stole from him years ago, desperately hoping that the baggy material would disguise the fact that I wasn't wearing a bra. I didn't have any other choice – I'd outgrown all of mine overnight. I was also secretly hoping that his fleeting scent that still lingered in the fabric would mask my newly acquired one.

I then grabbed the exact same pair of leggings that I'd worn yesterday from the floor and sniffed them to make sure they didn't smell, making a mental note to do a load of laundry when I got home tonight. I yanked them mercilessly over my enlarged hips before lacing up my beloved Nike Roshes and quietly tiptoeing down the stairs. I snatched an apple from the fruit bowl on our counter before I made a beeline towards the front door, trying my best to avoid being stopped by my mom - who I'm pretty sure was now awake and walking about upstairs if the creaking was any indication.

"Honey? Are you leaving for school already?" My mom's attempt at a sweet voice cascaded down the stairs. So close, I thought, letting out a sigh and closing the front door. I took a few steps further into the living room, but stayed far enough back so I would still be out of her line of sight.

"Yes, I was. Why?" I replied, annoyed. I watched as she made her way down the stairs and towards where I was leaning against the wall. It took everything in me not to roll my eyes at her. What was my deal this morning?

"Oh, no reason. Why are you in such a hurry? Usually you don't leave for school until you're already late." A light growl rumbled from my chest due to her accusing tone. Spinning on my heels, I opened the front door with more force than necessary.

"Because I have some research I need to finish for my biology project that's due at the end of the week. I'll see you later." I grumbled out the last part after I was already out the door, swiftly shutting it behind me before she could make another attempt at talking to me.

I reached the school minutes later - it was only a few blocks from my house - and I quickly found the library, claiming my usual desk. I frantically typed my question into the search engine on the exclusive werewolf website and began to read article after article, desperately trying to find anything that could provide me even the littlest of incite on my weird situation. I skimmed and scammed through the numerous paragraphs, but they all basically said the same thing; a female wolf only matured once she turned eighteen, never before. There wasn't any evidence that someone has ever matured before then, either.

"Well it must be possible because, well, hello? Here I am." I muttered to myself. I slumped back in the rolly chair with a frustrated sigh. This was supposed to help me, not further confuse me. I double-checked the built in calendar on the computer, which indeed read Tuesday January 2nd, 2016.

I was suddenly startled out of my confusion-induced haze as the bell indicating the ending of first period went off. I cussed under my breath, not even realizing how long I had unintentionally spent looking shit up. I swung my backpack over my shoulder and hesitated a few minutes before entering the hallway so that I came into contact with as few people as possible. It was nearly impossible to not notice the changes in my body, but I'll be damned if I wasn't going to try my best.

I quietly slipped into my second period classroom, ducking my head low and sliding into the last seat in the very back. I somehow managed to make myself nearly invisible, thank Goddess. Not even Kyler and Miller bothered me today. It was almost unnerving.

Popping the hood of my sweatshirt over my head, I made my way towards the cafeteria. I was 100% completely on edge because I knew that although I had managed to avoid everybody in my classes so far today, my luck wasn't going to continue through lunch. Especially if Savannah and her shit head minions had anything to do with it.

I pushed the doors to the cafeteria open and didn't even get to take two steps before every single set of eyes were on me. I glanced around, noticing a few males' nostrils flaring, obviously catching my scent.

"Fuck." I hissed under my breath. I knew it was going to be bad, but this was down right catastrophic. I cleared my throat and continued to make my way to the lunch line as if nothing had happened, but I couldn't block out the whispers. There were so many all at once that it was like a quite roar.

I finally took my seat beside Mickie, avoiding her piercing gaze that was burning a hole in the side of my face.

"Cece." She said pointedly. Her tone left no room for bull-shit.

"That's my name, don't wear it out." I replied sarcastically.

"Cut the shit and start talking." She demanded, narrowing her eyes at me.

"I don't know what you're talking about, Mickie." I spoke, trying to sound as unaffected as possible.

"I love to shop, but I'm not buying your bullshit." She said vehemently. I clenched my teeth to keep from laughing. I knew it would only serve to anger her more than she already was.

"Honestly, Mickie, it's been a long day already and I'm not in the mood for this. Can we please talk about something that matters for once?" I pleaded, completely exasperated. Instead of replying, she shook her head and rolled her eyes before opening her English book and resorting to completely ignoring me for the rest of lunch.

I effectively managed to avoid everyone for the majority of the rest of the week. I've only talked to my parents over text a few times since Tuesday morning. I would leave for school before either one of them woke up and stay at school until the bitchy librarian would finally kick me out - leaving me to wander around the woods before I knew my parents would be in bed and finally heading home. Whenever they would text me and ask me where I was or why I wasn't home, I would just use the excuse that I was hanging out with Mickie or working on final projects for school before the Mates Ball.

Now here I am, packing my suitcase for just that. I was peacefully listening to my Top 40 station on Pandora when my mother came barging into my room. I glanced at the clock in confusion. She shouldn't be home for another hour. The pack daycare must have let her off early for some reason.

"Cece are you almo-" Her sentence was cut short when she caught sight of me. Her eyes roamed over my body for the first time since I'd matured. The second I got home I ripped off my undergarments, deciding to go braless and panty-less while wearing my tank top and leggings. I just couldn't suffer any longer at the clutches of the one-size-too-small bra I had borrowed from Mickie and underwear that dug into my skin. I rested my hands on my gigantic hips and cocked my eyebrow up in question. I don't know why she was surprised. This morning was the morning that I was supposed to mature. It was almost like she had forgotten...

"You look so diff-"

"Yes I'm almost done packing. Just need to grab my tooth brush and tooth paste." I said, once again cutting her off, but also answering her first question. Not letting people finish their sentences seemed to be my thing as of lately.

"Okay sweetheart. When you're finished, Leighton is wait- ing downstairs with the car warm and ready." She said before giving me one last faint smile and ducking out the door. A tinge of guilt stabbed my heart from the way I was treating her, but my wolf just huffed it off.

I had almost forgotten that Leighton was the one taking me. He wasn't exempt from my list of people I'd been ignoring all week. I sent all of his calls to voicemail and deleted his texts without even reading them. I knew I was being petty, but I didn't give a shit. I'm pretty sure he got the message that I was pissed at him. Good.

I ignored all of Leighton's attempts at conversation while lugging my stuff into the trunk of his black Escalade. Instead, I let my mind wander to how nice it was going to be when we got to the island where everything was taking place. I didn't know the exact name of the island, but it's said that the council bought it for the specific reason of constructing a giant ass building to hold all the wolves in the U.S. at one time. Leighton yelling my name cut off my peaceful daydreams of the sunny beach where I would lay on a towel tanning.

"What!" I snapped at him over my shoulder.

"I asked what the hell your problem was. You've been ignoring me all damn week!" He yelled, clearly frustrated. I had to hold back my giggle. I always found it amusing when Alphas threw temper tantrums whenever they didn't get what they wanted. So amusing.

"You sure are a genius, aren't you?" I stated, sarcasm dripping from my words. He let a threatening growl rumble from his chest at my disrespectful tone. My wolf didn't even flinch. Weird.

"Care to enlighten me?" He asked while we both buckles our seatbelts.

"I just don't associate myself with liars is all." I jeered, trying to sound as unaffected as possible. I didn't need him knowing

I had taken his side over my parents'. I was still ticked at him for not telling me the whole truth. I glanced at him from my peripheral and took note of how the color seemed to have completely drained from his face. Furrowing my eyebrows in confusion, I turned my body so I was now facing him head on.

"I don't know what you're talking about." He said, lying through his teeth. I could tell by the way he shifted his eyes between the red light ahead of us and me.

"So you offered to escort me to the Mate's Ball? It wasn't Alpha's orders?" I challenged him. I noticed we had already pulled up to the airport and had parked.

"Look, Aceso-"

"Save it." I growled out, swinging my door open and escaping before he could try and spin his words to convince me that he didn't lie to me in the first place.

That asshole can get all of our luggage by himself. Serves him right.

By the time our plane had finally landed on the island, I was exhausted. Not just from the jetlag I was experiencing, but also from having to deal with the entire group of asshole jocks that thought it was okay to harass me while Leighton and I were waiting for our connecting flight. A shiver of disgust ran through me when I thought of all their futile attempts at "flirting" with me.

Who the fuck finds the name "sweet bottom" appealing? Dear God. I huffed to myself. My wolf growled in agreement.

I quickly found my way to the hotel type room I would be staying in for the next few days. I began to notice my wolf's growing restlessness ever since we got off the plane. I shook it off, pegging it down as needing sleep before climbing into bed and falling asleep almost instantly.

Chapter 3

Alethia's POV

I passed by the desolate door like I have every day for the past eighteen years of my life. Stopping midstride, I turned around and leisurely made my way back towards it. I chewed on my bottom lip, a nervous habit I've had ever since I was just a little girl. I examined the dust-caked white wooden door. The room hasn't been touched since she was taken.

I can recall the last time someone had spoken about the taboo that was this room and the life that had once inhabited it. It had been an Alpha that was visiting from a neighboring pack, an ally of ours. He'd noticed the room's abandoned state on the way to my father's office and decided to make a comment about fixing the room up to be an office for our Beta. He thought it was only logical because, well, no one was using it. No one had ever really used it.

My father killed him then and there. Slit his throat with a single claw and walked away as if it was just another mundane task - like doing laundry or cooking dinner. He ordered Beta Aaron to explain the situation to the diseased Alpha's pack on his behalf and instructed him to give them the choice to join ours, or go rogue.

I was nine years old then.

It was the first time I can remember being so absolutely terrified of my father, the man who salved my tears and bandaged my scraped knees.

It was times like that, that took me back to when my parents first told me about my long lost sister. It was about a week after my sixth birthday had passed. My mother physically couldn't do it, the words had escaped her completely - my father was no better. He struggled to finish his sentences, and when he did they were clipped and dripping with sorrow and pain. He had held my small frame that resided on his lap so tight it was painful, but I thought better than to say anything. It was as if he thought that the second he loosened the vice grip he had on me, I would disappear into thin air.

They'd then proceeded to show me pictures that were captured during the short three months they were blessed to spend with the both of us. My chest ached with the happiness they radiated in every single one. I'd never seen them smile so immense before - like they were in those pictures. Being so young and innocent when they told me, I wasn't able to comprehend why someone would want to sneak through our window, into our once shared room, and snatch my baby sister right out from under my parents' noses.

Things were never the same.

It was as if a giant storm cloud had rolled in over our entire pack, never leaving or letting up; just ominously hanging there, causing a grey cast over everything that was once sunny and bright. Dulling the life in each and every pack members' eyes.

I feverishly wiped at the one traitorous tear that rolled down my cheek. I heard the telltale creek of the floorboards as someone walked up behind me. My father's familiar scent of aftershave and pine trees engulfed me like a warm blanket. His presence, although comforting, only seemed to make my throat constrict even more as I tried to hold back a sob that was so dangerously close to breaking free.

Sensing my obvious emotional distress, he wound his arms around my much smaller frame and tugged me back against his chest while resting his chin on my forehead. I silently shook as he tried to calm me down.

"I should of tried harder. Looked farther. I never should have given up. I failed her." His deep, rich voice was barely above a whisper and so unbelievably broken that it made me cry harder.

"Y-you did everything you c-could, Dad. Everyone did. I don't ever want to hear you s-say that again." I choked out angrily through my tears. I didn't mean for it to be so harsh, but it tore me up inside knowing he blamed himself. He always has, and probably always will. He sees it as his inability to keep his den safe and also failing to protect his pups from harm. That's hard on any father, but it's even worse for wolves. Our pups were everything to us.

"I don't want you leaving tonight. If preventing you from going wasn't illegal, and the council wouldn't come after me, I'd keep you here and you wouldn't be attending this stupid ball." I let out a frustrated sigh at his statement.

"Not this again. You and mom will both be there. As Alpha and Luna, your attendance is required. I will be safe. No one is going to take me. As far as finding my mate goes, I don't think he would put up a fight against you making him transfer to our pack, Dad. You've acquired quite the reputation over the years." I jibbed before lightly bumping his shoulder with my own. He chuckled at this and I couldn't help but let out a relieved breath. Once he got into one of his moods, nothing could get him out of it except for spending hours in solitude with my mother. And sometimes, not even that would help. His eyes suddenly glazed over and I waited until he was done responding to whomever was mind linking him.

"That was Xavier. I have a meeting with him that started five minutes ago." His face turned grim and I knew exactly what the meeting was about without even having to ask.

"Dad, you can't force a grown ass man to go to the Mate's Ball if he doesn't want to. Besides, he's a Wild. If you expect him to take a plane to an isolated island just to parade around a fancy room amongst a bunch of people he doesn't know when he can barely speak fluent English anymore, you're dumber than I thought. He's already refused four times. I guarantee you that asking a fifth time isn't going to make him change his mind." I said, slight annoyance lacing my tone. Through the last two years, I've learned Xavier well enough to be able to understand his moods and also his wolf tongue. We didn't need to exchange flimsy words, but when we did, they were usually important.

"I know, I know my sweet angel, but I will always have my pack members best interests in mind. I can see the way he acts when he thinks no one is watching. His shoulders slump and his eyes get this dead look. The only reason he stays living is because we have a deeply rooted respect for each other ever since he saved my ass all those months back. He sticks around to protect our family as well as the pack, because he knows what its like to lose everything and he loves this pack like his own. I just want him to be happy, Alethia. Everyone deserves to be happy, as well as have a chance to love and be loved." I nodded, tears forming in my eyes once again from his beautiful words.

"I've also considered naming him my successor. Since your mother and I were never able to conceive again, there isn't a male to take over. I'm getting old, and your mother wants to spend more time together. As her mate, I want to give her that - especially after everything that we've been through as a family. It's about time somebody better suited for the job takes over, and Xavier is more than qualified. I just need to ensure I give the search for his mate my all before I hand my title down to him."

I was more than surprised by what he just told me. He's never even hinted at possibly giving Xavier his Alpha title. I could see why he would want to, but there's no way people would feel 100% comfortable and at ease around him, unless he had someone to smooth out all his rough edges. I didn't know what to say to him, so I simply nodded. Leaning up on my tiptoes, I planted a firm kiss against his stubbly cheek. I turned back around once again and made my way to my room to finish packing before I ran out of time.

"Do you want some help, dear?" My mothers soothing voice called out from the doorway.

"Would you mind? I can never get this fucking zipper closed!" I huffed while pushing down forcefully on the top of my suitcase.

"Language, young lady!" She scolded, smacking me upside the head and making us both giggle in the process. There was a pregnant pause before she raised her eyebrow at me in a questioning manner.

"What's the matter my child?" She asked, resting her hands over top my own (which were still tugging furiously at the stuck zipper). She knew me better than I even knew myself. This worked against me more often than not.

"Do you... Do you think she could be there? I mean, she'd be eighteen now. No matter where she is, no one can avoid the council when it comes to attending the Mate's Ball." I spoke timidly, knowing that she had, without a doubt, considered that very same thing at least once within the last month.

"Alethia, enough. I don't want to hear another word." She snapped. I could hear the hurt in her voice, but I couldn't bring myself to feel guilty. I missed her too. Being a twin, I can vaguely feel the special bond we share pulse just underneath my skin. Although incredibly weak, it was still there.

"But mom you're not even listening to me!" I said, beginning to raise my voice. I was exasperated at this point. She never wanted to talk about this. She'd rather sweep it under the rug and deal with her emotions behind closed doors all on her own.

"No! You're wrong, Alethia Rose! I am hearing every single word you're saying, but I have gotten my hopes up so many times just to be disappointed time and time again! I'm done with hope, now enough with the foolishness. When you're ready, your father and I will be waiting for you in the car." I plopped down on the end of my bed and crossed my arms. It took everything in me to keep my tongue and not lash out at her.

"Fine." I said as she slammed the door behind her.

So much for helping me I guess.

I stretched my cramped muscles before stepping off of the plane. Letting out a large yawn, I glanced around before spotting Xavier's gigantic form looming over everyone else's while standing next to his luggage. His arms were crossed and his body was rigid as always. He stood ramrod straight while continuously scanning the crowd of people around him. He was the most observant person I've ever come across in my entire life. It was almost comical how even most Alpha's that arrived took one look at his stoic expression and warily kept their distance.

I was still damn surprised that my father managed to talk him into coming. I wonder what magic tale he had to spin to make it happen.

I cautiously made my way towards him, ensuring he would notice me before I got too close. He tends to get quite jumpy and almost always acts on impulse. He almost beheaded our best pack doctor on accident two months ago.

Finally standing next to him, I had to force my wolf down. This happen almost every time we were in each other's company. It was mainly because he exuded so much power it was unsettling for my naturally dominant wolf and she felt the need to make her presence known.

Although all odds were against our friendship, we still got on really well. Our wolves had a general understanding for one another and the loss that the both of us have been through.

"That flight was about as pleasant as listening to Rachel Finland talk about her self." I mumbled when glanced at me with an expectant look. This was how it always was; I started the conversation and he would vaguely respond. I could see the amusement spark in his eyes at my comment, but that was it. The entire time I had known the guy, I'd never heard a single laugh, or even seen a single smile, from him. His impassive gaze was the one he sported 24/7 and it usually kept people away, but that was the way he liked it.

I searched his face while he was staring off in the distance, looking deep in thought about something or other. He had noticeable purple bags under his eyes that even my M.A.C. prolong wear concealer couldn't cover, and his face was covered in a 5 o'clock shadow. My wolf whimpered sadly for her friend.

Xavier was already 25 and had still yet to find his mate, obviously. Most people who don't found their mate after roughly two years of turning legal age usually never found their mate. It was rare, but it was the harsh reality some wolves had to face. I couldn't help the surge of anger I felt toward the Moon Goddess for not giving Xavier this one thing. He had been through so much shit in his life. He protected those he cared for fiercely, that much was shown through the numerous white gashes that littered his chest and back, and he deserved so much more than the hand he's been dealt.

"It's late and we've got a big day ahead of us tomorrow. Get some sleep, okay?" I said softly. He gave me a single terse nod before roughly grabbing his single duffle bag and heading for the male sector of the large hotel-like building. I watched closely to see if I could witness the way he carried himself like my dad had said. Sure enough, his back hunched over and he began dragging his feet as he walked.

I said a silent prayed to the Moon for my future Alpha before taking my own advice and settling into bed, anxious for what tomorrow might bring.

Chapter 4

Aceso's POV

I lunged for the microwave and yanked the door open as stealthily as I could before it beeped. I smirked and patted myself on the back as the timer read 00:00.

Nailed it.

Leaning my back against the kitchen island, I brought the mug of warmed up milk to my lips. I took a greedy sip and nearly moaned at the comforting taste that encased my mouth. Ever since I was a little girl, this was the only thing that could ease my restlessness enough to help me fall sleep.

Because I was lost in my lactose-induced paradise, I hadn't heard the quiet shuffling of feet on the kitchen tiles coming towards me.

"Mind if I join your one woman party?" A sweet feminine voice spoke out behind me. Startled, I whipped around - effectively splashing my milk all over my pajamas - and cursed under my breath. I glanced up, finally getting a good look at her. The second our eyes met, an unusual warmth spread throughout my chest, but it disappeared before I could identify its origin. My wolf whimpered once before settling down.

"If you did, then it wouldn't be a one woman party, now would it?" I teased, the edges of my lips pulling up into a playful smirk. She giggled at my comment and then focused her eyes on the cup I had cradled in my hand.

"Is that-"

"Warm milk." We said at the same time.

"Jinx!" We then both yelled again. A few seconds of silence passed between us before we burst out laughing. She shushed me between giggles, no doubt trying to keep us from waking up every she-wolf in the building; or even worse, one of the Alpha couples that were chaperoning us.

"So, you can't sleep either?" She questioned before occupying the barstool directly across the counter from where I was standing. I nodded, grabbing the gallon that I had just put back in the refrigerator mere minutes ago and began to warm her up a cup of her own, sensing that was her reason for being down in the kitchen in the first place.

"Not at all. My wolf has been restless ever since we arrived. It was only when she started whining that I knew there was no way in hell I was getting any shut eye without a little cat beer." I said, nudging my head at my half empty cup that now rested on the granite top.

"No way! You call it that too? I thought it was just me and my dad!" She exclaimed, excitement gleaming in her eyes. I couldn't help but smile along with her as I handed over her own mug, careful not to burn myself.

"I read it on this website once when I was like ten and it's stuck with me ever since. My parents nearly shit their pants when I said it. They interrogated me for nearly an hour trying to figure out where I learned what beer was. I guess it never dawned on them that I didn't actually know." I rolled my eyes as the memory faded into the recesses of my mind once again. She snorted in response before a comfortable silence ascended between us.

I was amazed how easy it was to talk to her. She was a complete stranger yet I was getting along with her better than I ever got along with Mickie sometimes. I didn't even know her name, but I felt as if we've known each other our whole lives. She even managed to somewhat calm my wolf's unease.

I studied her features while she graciously sipped her drink. Her pin straight, midnight black hair fell just slightly past her shoulders, and she had these absolutely stunning emerald green eyes that were framed by thick black eyelashes. She looked like she belonged on a runway in Milan or Paris. I was instantly envious of her unreal cheekbones; they were so sharp, I'm pretty sure they could cut a bitch.

"What's your name?" I blurted. I felt the strange need to know more about the stranger in front of me.

"Alethia, but most people call me Lee for short. What about you?"

"Aceso, but most call me Cece. What pack are you from?" I prayed in my head that her pack wasn't too far from mine - I would love to hangout with her again. Mainly because I didn't get along with many people, so I wanted to hold on to this newfound friendship for as long as I possibly could. I saw the hesitation in her eyes and felt horrible for making her uncomfortable with my abrupt interrogation.

"I'm so sorry, I didn't mean to pry." I rushed out, my cheeks heating up the slightest bit with embarrassment.

"No, no. You're fine. It's just that my pack doesn't really have the best...reputation if you will. Most people tend to run for the hills when they find out where I'm from and who I am." I furrowed my eyebrows in confusion and waited for her to elaborate.

"My parents are the Alpha and Luna of Bloodlust pack." I gasped at her admission, which caused her to squirm uncomfortably. I'd heard all the 'horror' stories of what her pack has done to others. They exterminated rogues the second they stepped foot on to their land, and they never showed mercy to anyone. I've also heard that they're incredibly loyal to their pack members and protect their own with a fierceness that one could only wish for from an Alpha couple.

"No shit?! Your mom and dad are, like, totally fucking kick-ass!" I exclaimed. Her eyes widened in shock before she threw her head back and laughed.

"Well, that's definitcly a new one. Most people tell me all about how we're nothing but cold-hearted murderers. You should totally meet them some time. They'd love you!" She squealed, getting overly excited. My smile faded and I audibly gulped. Talking to their daughter was one thing, but actually meeting the legendary Bloodlust Alpha and Luna was a whole other thing entirely.

I let out a large yawn and glanced at the clock, shocked that I had already been down here with her for an hour, just simply talking and getting to know each other. I was saddened to know that this vacation, if you will, was most likely the only time we would get to spend together. Our packs hated each other, though nobody but the higher-ranks and pack elders knew exactly why.

"Well, I think I'm going to head to bed now and salvage what little sleep I can. I'll see you tomorrow morning?" I asked in a hopeful tone. She nodded her head enthusiastically and gave me a friendly smile as I set my now empty cup in the sink. The milk had definitely served its purpose, because the second my head hit my pillow; I was out like a light.

I peeped my eyes open, only to groan and squeeze them shut once again in an attempt to avoid the blaring sun that had seeped through my window blinds. I rolled over on the decently sized tempurpedic mattress and examined the clock that was hung on the wall above the dresser. I was still pissed at the sun for waking me up, but at least I would still make it in time for breakfast.

After replacing my milk stained shirt with the first article of clothing I found in my suitcase, I exited my room and began navigating my way towards the giant dining room they'd pointed out when we had all arrived yesterday. I felt someone's presence behind me and peeked over my shoulder to see Alethia in the same shape that I was currently in: messy bed hair, crinkled clothes, and sporting a tired scowl that very clearly said "don't fuck with me". I slowed my pace so that we soon fell instep with each other.

"Who the hell invented mornings in the first place?" She grumbled, her voice scratchy from sleep. I giggled at her rhetorical question.

"Probably the same person who invented geometry and raisins." I answered. She nodded her head while scrunching her nose up before we fell into another comfortable silence, similar to the one in the kitchen last night. As we passed quite a few other females one our way, I couldn't help the question that tumbled from my mouth.

"Have you seen a single male since you got here? I swear it's like none of them bothered to show up. The amount of estrogen in this place is starting to suffocate me." She turned her head to look at me, confusion written all over her face.

"What are you talking about? The males and females are always split up until the actual event. It's been that way ever since the very beginning. It's to ensure that some desperate male wolf doesn't claim what isn't his. The only males permitted in our wing are the mated Alphas because they can't be separated from their mates. That and so they can protect us." I was surprised at how thoughtful the werewolf council actually was when it came to these sorts of things. I would've never thought about the possibility of someone committing such a heinous crime – which is exactly what falsely claiming a female was.

"Logical enough." I replied as we reached a set of large double doors. The second we stepped into the room, the most delicious aroma invaded my senses. It was borderline orgasmic.

"Bacon." Alethia and I simultaneously moaned.

"JINX!" We yelled together - yet again – as the both of us tried to one-up the other. I heard a deep chuckle from somewhere in the room. Alethia and I's heads turned in the general direction from which it came. My eyes immediately widened and I snapped my head towards the floor, baring my neck to the incredibly Alpha before me. I squeezed my eyes shut and silently prayed that he wasn't one of those power-greedy assholes who liked to make "examples" of those who disobeyed common werewolf laws. My wolf growled loudly at me in the back of my head and I winced.

What the fuck does she think she's doing? I thought to myself. She barked at me furiously, upset with my actions. Why was she mad at me for submitting to someone of higher status? She knows better than to push me to question the authority of those above me – I still have a few whipping scars on my back from learning that lesson the hard way.

"ACESO!" I was abruptly pulled from my internal conversation with myself and looked up to see Alethia looking at me with confusion yet again written all over her face.

"Sorry, what did you say?" I asked sheepishly.

"I said, I wanted to introduce you to my dad, Alpha Jerrod Nightly." I could hear the pride in her voice as she gestured towards the very Alpha I had accidentally had a stare down with.

"Alpha." I said, bowing my head in a gesture of respect. He chuckled at my antics and waved his hand in the air, as if dismissing the formal greeting.

"Please, call me Jerrod. Any friend of Alethia's is a friend of mine. I insist you have a seat and join us!" I was shocked at how friendly he was, especially because I was a Nightshade member. His tone left no room for negotiation, not that

I would have declined anyway. I was in the presence of a fucking legend.

I piled my plate high with food and instantly dug in, letting out a relieved sign as I got a taste of the delicious food. Alethia and I would tease each other between bites of food, occasionally shoving our shoulders against the other and then giggling like crazy afterwards when it caused the other's food to fall off their fork. I could feel a penetrating gaze the entire time we were eating, and I knew it was Alpha Jerrod. I figured he was just assessing me to make sure I was of no threat to his daughter.

What surprised me the most was that the longer I was around him, the more comfortable I became? Being an omega, the mere presence of one, let alone two, Alphas was usually enough to have my wolf howling in my head. I was midsentence when Alpha Jerrod cut me off.

"I'm sorry, I know you said you were from Nightshade Pack, but are you sure you're an omega?" His eyes narrowed as they scanned my face, as if searching for something.

"Yes, Alp-um-Jerrod. Well, at least since I last checked." I joked. He let out a gruff laugh at my reply, but I could still see the curiosity gleaming in his intense eyes.

"Anyway, Aceso, I was going to ask you if you wanted to get ready with me tonight? My mom might will be there too, so you could meet her then!" Alethia said with renewed vigor. I couldn't help but grin from ear-to-ear as well as share her giddy mood. I'd never gotten ready with a close girlfriend before, but from all the cliché human preteen movies I've seen throughout the years. It's apparently a crucial life experience one must experience. I nodded my head heartily and she squealed loudly while clapping her hands.

"Here's what's going on, buddy: the day we get married is the day I ship those brats off to Switzerland, get the picture? It's me, or them. Take your pick." I quoted with the snobbiest accent I could muster. Alethia laughed so hard she had tears rolling down her face. We both threw our hands up and let out a victorious yell when Hallie and Annie's dad picked them, duh, over that evil witch Meredith.

"TAKE THAT, BITCH!" Alethia exclaimed, which then lead to a whole new round of giggles.

"Your dad is amazing." I randomly blurted as the credits began to roll.

"Yeah, he really is. But dear Goddess he can be so overprotective sometimes. He made me wear fucking pool floaties while swimming until I was, like, eight." I snickered at her expense, unable to imagine her in a one piece swimming suit and little plastic arm floaters.

"Well, at least you actually get along with your parents. I swear, mine breathe and I get annoyed. I went through this phase when I was little where the only thing I wanted was a sibling. I would ask them every day, multiple times a day, when I was getting a little brother or sister. They would always give me the same bullshit excuse. "You're just so perfect that we don't need to have another kid. You're enough for us!" I mocked. I heard a sniffle and I looked at Alethia, concern flooding my entire being when I saw the tears that had gathered in her eyes. I shot up in my seat, about to ask her what was wrong, but before I could she began to tell me.

"I had a sister. A twin. Our cribs were in the same room because I guess we were inseparable. Every time they would move us even an inch away from the other, we would scream our lungs out." She smiled at the fond memory and continued. "When we were just three months old, someone got through our border patrol and kidnapped her right out from under our noses. They didn't even suspect a thing. It wasn't until an hour later when I had woken up and became restless that they discovered what had happened. It tore the entire pack apart, but it took the biggest toll on my dad. He still blames himself to this day for her disappearance. He's so sad all the time. Today during breakfast is the first time I've seen him genuinely smile and laugh in years." By the end of her heartbreaking confession we were both sobbing messes. I pulled her into a tight hug and squeezed her hard until our tears finally subsided, wishing that maybe we could have been related in a different life.

Chapter 5

Alpha Jerrod's POV

Folding my hands in my lap, I leaned forward and placed my elbows on my thighs as I watched Alethia and her new friend getting ready. Most would find it creepy, but I can't find it in me to let my daughter out of my sight. Not when we're on unfamiliar land that I can't navigate easily. And just like every time before, a searing pain shot straight through my heart at the thought of my lost daughter. We hadn't even had a chance to name her, or Alethia yet.

I let out a strained laugh at the memory of my beautiful wife, Lidia, and I arguing over what we were going to name our two angels. We'd struggled for two years to conceive - so imagine our surprise when the doctor told us we were having twins. We were completely overjoyed. It was one of the only times in my life I had ever cried. That of course, was before everything happened.

They were our little miracles, and we cherished them with everything we had the second they came into this world. We didn't want to give them ordinary names, because the elders had said they could tell our girls were destined for great things.

It wasn't until a few weeks after our child was taken that one of our highly respected elders had named Alethia with our consent. We fell in love with the name instantly. I suggested that we name our other bundle of joy, but every time I brought the subject up, Lidia would shut me out and refuse to speak to me. I tried to be strong for my mate, I really did, but the grief eventually got to me and I cracked. I locked away all my emotions and killed anyone who dared step foot on my land without my permission first. I refused to let another one of my pack families go through what my family and I had.

Pushing away the painful memories, I was jerked back to reality when Aceso let out a loud, boisterous laugh. I couldn't help but be taken aback by how similar it was to Lidia's. They almost sounded identical. It always amazed me how such a large sound could be projected from such a little body. My wolf began pacing in my head, whining and pawing at me to let him forward, but I didn't have a clue as to why.

I tried to ignore it and focus on my precious little girl and how happy she looked. I've heard her laugh more in the last day than I have her entire life. Her and this new girl, Aceso, talked and joked as if they'd known each other their whole life. What shocked me even more, was that Alethia knew that this girl was a Nightshade, but she didn't seem to care one bit. If she did, she didn't show it at all.

"Hey, Lee, is there any chance you brought a second dress with you? I didn't even think to buy a new dress after I matured because I was so stressed with...uh...school." I looked up at her and studied her face with narrowed eyes, not missing the fact that she hesitated on her words.

"Of course! Lucky for you we're basically the same size. Here!" Aceso's eyes lite up as she gazed at the dress, and I couldn't keep the smile from my face. The warm feeling in my chest was the exact same as whenever Alethia smiled or did something that made me proud. It was unnerving in the slightest.

"Speaking of which, how was your maturation? I swear to God, if mine was anything like how childbirth is going to be, I'm adopting." Alethia said with a huff, causing me to laugh. I distinctly remember her screams of pain and harsh words directed at anything and everything just about a week ago. Aceso seemed to become extremely uncomfortable with the question and began to fidget.

She audibly gulped before saying, "Well, actually, I sort of – um - matured early I guess?" She squeaked out. My brows shot up in surprise and confusion. I've never heard of a female maturing early. I don't think it's ever happened before. Matter of fact, I'm positive it hasn't. As an Alpha, we're required to read general history records about our species. That type of thing never came up.

"What? That's impossible!" Alethia exclaimed, voicing my exact thoughts.

"That's what I thought too. I'm not sure why, or how it happened, but it did. My birthday was actually yesterday, but I matured Monday morning around 6 something in the morning. It was the weirdest thing ever. I thought I was dying at first." She said, a visible shiver of fear coursing down her spine. My breath caught in my throat as it tightened, constricting my airway. There's no way...

"Wait a minute...did...did you say Monday?" Alethia asked skeptically. I could see the wheels turning in her head and I was positive she was thinking the same thing I was. I instantly mind linked my wife to come to Alethia's room at once, letting her now how urgent the situation was with my tone. There were just far too many coincidences for me to overlook the situation in front of me.

"Yeah. Well, anyway, to answer your question - my maturation sucked. The most excruciatingly painful thing I've ever been through. Worse than my first shift, and I didn't even think that was physically possible. I'll be right back, I'm going to go put this on." She said, gesturing towards the dress in her hands. Neither Alethia nor I said anything in response. I couldn't find the words. Just as I heard the bathroom door click shut, the familiar scent of lavender surrounded me.

"Does someone want to tell me what the hell is going on? Why do you two look like you've seen a ghost?" Lidia demanded.

"My love, you may want to sit down for this." I whispered softly, my heart beating a mile a minute.

Aceso's POV

I successfully managed to zip the back of the dress before turning to examine myself in the mirror. It dress suited my body perfectly. It was a bright, fuchsia pink A-Line style gown with off-the-shoulder sleeves and a fitted bodice. The color looked amazing with my new tan and bright hair. I had no doubt that this gorgeous gown was expensive as hell after I fingered the fabric with my hands. It was definitely made of the best silk. I felt guilty just by trying it on, let alone wearing it, but I knew that money wasn't even a thought to Alethia and her family. Word on the street was, her pack was absolutely loaded. Alpha Jerrod was very smart with his investments. Or so I've heard.

The sound of knuckles hitting wood brought me to my senses. A door was slammed shut and a silky female voice flowed through the room that connected to the bathroom I was currently in. It sounded like Alethia's, but more mature. I had no doubt that it was her mother. Butterflies began to swarm my stomach and I clenched my hands together in front of me.

What if she doesn't like me?

I took a few deep breaths before smoothing out the front of my dress and reached for the door. The second I came into view, all eyes were on me. My eyes met the Luna and I gasped. It was as if I was looking at a picture of myself twenty years from now. We stood at the same height, had the same round face shape, same crystal blue eyes, and the same long blonde tresses. The only minor difference was that my hair was almost white, where as hers was more of a golden shade.

Nobody spoke, but I knew that I wasn't the only one who had noticed the unusualness of the situation. Suddenly, the woman before me began to sob into her hand. The sight of the Luna crying sent my wolf on a rampage. She began to bark at me over and over again, but I had no idea what it was she was trying to tell me. I focused harder, finally seeing the image of a woman cradling a baby. Then, it hit me like a sack of bricks. My throat tightened and tears of my own began to form.

She's showing me a mom...

"M-mommy?" I choked out, barely above a whisper. Seconds later, I was pulled into a bone crushing hug as she began to run her hand through the hair at the back of my head.

"My baby girl. Oh, my beautiful angel!" She repeated the words over and over again, never letting up on her suffocating grip. I couldn't stop the tears from flowing freely now. Nothing made sense, but the one thing I knew for sure was that this was where I belonged.

I pulled away from her before peeking over her shoulder to see my father, my real father, staring at me with nothing but love and adoration in his tear-clouded eyes. I broke away from my mom and ran at him, jumping into his arms.

"Daddy." I cried as he clutched at my body for dear life. His body shook lightly as he tried to contain his sobs, but he wasn't fooling me.

"Seventeen years and six months is how long I've searched for you, my angel." His voice cracked before trailing off at the end.

"I'm here. I'm right here. I'm not going anywhere." I assured him over and over.

"Fuck you guys! I had my smokey eye perfect for ONCE and here I am a smeared mess." Alethia complained, her voice thick with emotion. I laughed whole-heartedly before pulling my sister into a tight embrace.

"All this time I had a sister and I didn't even know it. This is almost as good as finding my mate would be." I said, my words coming out slightly muffled because my face was buried against Alethia's shoulder.

"Almost? You asshole, we're twins! Where's the bond sympathy, sister!" She exclaimed, feigning irritation. I laughed as our mom scolded her for the foul language.

"I need to inform Xavier about everything that's happened sometime tonight. Girls, I need you to listen to me very carefully. You are not to go anywhere unless I am with you for the remainder of this trip, and I expect you both to stay by my side all night. Understood?" He spoke sternly. I nodded my head, agreeing with his demands.

"Who's Xavier?" I questioned, unable to contain my curiosity.

"Our hot as hell future Alpha, well my dad hasn't actually asked him yet, but I know he'll accept. He's not my mate, but Goddess bless whoever's mate he is." I squealed at her statement.

"I can't wait to meet him!" I suggestively replied, winking at Lee as we laughed together.

"Alright my beauties, we can all discuss what we're going to do about Aceso's fake parents later, but we only have thirty minutes before we need to meet up with the rest of our group. I'll come and get you when we're done, Jerrod." She said dismissively, causing him to raise an eyebrow at her defiantly.

"If you think I'm leaving for even a second, you're insane my love. Now that I have all my girls in one room, there's not a damn thing in this world that's going to get me out of here." We all giggled at the determined look on his face, which made his smile broaden.

"If you say so. Well, lets get to work!" My mom exclaimed excitedly as she ushered Alethia and I back into the bathroom.

Chapter 6

Xavier's POV

Beep. Beep. Beep.

I released a deep sigh as I slammed my hand on the alarm clock, trying to turn the annoying piece of shit off. Growing increasingly frustrated, I ripped the small piece of plastic from the wall and chucked it across the room as hard as I could, effectively shattering it into a million tiny pieces.

Running my hands down my face, I groaned. Yet another sleepless night I thought to myself as I stared up at the plain white ceiling. The bed was warm and comfortable. The temperature in the room was perfect: not too warm, not too cold, and the room was silent enough. This was definitely favorable to the normal hard forest floor that I normally sleep on in wolf form. There was no reason I shouldn't have been able to fall asleep. But, there was one thing that had made it impossible to get more than a couple hours of undisturbed slumber at one time.

As cliché as it sounds, it's my thoughts that keep me up at night. The constant wondering of where she is, what she's possibly doing, if she's even still alive. What she might look like. Is her hair long or short? Are her eyes a dark, rich brown that glow in the sun? Or are they a crystal clear blue that could take my breath away and suck me in like a tidal wave. Will she have freckles? Is she tall or short?

My mind runs ramped with all the possibilities. I know that no matter what she looks like, I would love her with everything I have. The throbbing pain in my chest increased with every breath I took. My wolf was abnormally restless compared to what he normally is when we first wakeup. It was probably just because we weren't used to being in our skin form. It wasn't uncomfortable, just awkward. I often found it hard to communicate properly after not being in this form after extended periods of time.

I swiftly sat up and threw my legs over the side of my bed as I let out an annoyed growl for what seemed to be no particular reason; the wolf was just extra snarky today I guess. Showering quickly, I threw on my usual outfit when I took this form; a simple black T-shirt, dark wash jeans, and a pair of timberlands, which were a gift from Alpha Jerrod's kind mate. My wolf always took an extra liking to her in what I understood as a motherly sense.

Mornings like these were the worst. The incredible longing for my mate only got worse over time, and always brought back memories of my past with it. They weren't memories I ever wanted to relive. I wish I could just forget them all together, but I know that's impossible.

My wolf began growling in the back of my head at detour that my thoughts began to take. I missed my parents more than anything. They were strong, fierce leaders who never backed down from a fight. That was ultimately what got them killed. Our pack never saw the attack coming. It was in the middle of the night and came without warning. I'd never seen so many rogue wolves together in one place ever before in my life.

Everybody in our pack fought long and hard, but in the end it just wasn't enough. We'd managed to kill every single rogue, but all that was left of my pack was myself along with about twelve other pack members. All of which were unmated males, like myself. I was twenty-two at the time the attack took place and had only been leading for a little over a year. My members were all wary about me running the pack alone without my Luna by my side, of course, but I had proven myself to them numerous times and had easily gained their unwavering loyalty.

I blamed myself because they misplaced their trust in me and I failed them all. The constant burden hung on my shoulders ever since that night. I never wanted to be involved in pack life ever again because I didn't want to screw something up somehow and make someone else go through what I did. That's why I was so hesitant to Alpha Jerrod's offer to join his pack after first saving him, but he insisted. Once I got to know the man for more than the label he holds, we discovered that we had something major in common – we had both lost an extremely dear person in our lives. That was when I decided that this was going to be my way of redeeming myself and making my parents proud. I was going to watch over Jarrod's pack and make sure nothing ever harmed them ever again.

tI would always hold a special place in my heart for Alpha Jerrod and his wonderful mate. When I finally shifted and told them of the tragedy that my remaining pack member's and I had been through, they welcomed me, as well as all my surviving men, with open arms. The gesture surprised everyone. Even surrounding packs – or so I heard. Bloodlust been known to kill anyone who wasn't their own ever since their daughter had been taken. I wasn't too keen on having to answer to someone after being an alpha myself, especially because I had taken an extreme liking to being a Wild, but I was immediately given the position of head warrior alongside their current one. I trained all of Alpha Jarrod's men in war form and had significantly improved their fighting tactics over the last couple of years.

I hadn't realized how long I had been thinking for until I finally reached the dining hall. I ducked under the doorframe to avoid hitting my head and strode over to the designated table for high-ranking wolves.

Although I didn't have an official title, no one dared speak out against me. Smart. Scanning my eyes across everyone who sat before me, I could blatantly see the fear instilled in their orbs due to my presence. I refrained from smirking at their expense, knowing it wouldn't be a wise decision. I began to eat in silence, as always, enjoying the decent enough breakfast that had been presented to me. I was almost finished when a loud commotion from the corner of the room caught my attention.

I recognized the two wolves instantly by their scent. The taller and older of the two was that bastard Alpha Jack of

Nightshade. I know I haven't met the boy he's speaking with, but I'm sure by the resemblances they share, that it must be his son. I've only spoken with Alpha Jack a handful of times, but I really only needed to meet him just once to know that he was a huge dick head. He tried to act as if he was superior to everyone he surrounded himself with, but, in all honesty, he was a terrible Alpha. As was his father. The apple doesn't fall far from the tree, they say.

It's no secret that he treats his lower-ranks like scum that you get on the bottom of your shoe, and the way he's trained his warriors is flat out comical. I've called him out on it only once before. It was the first time I spoke in my skin form in front of anyone since the accident. I know for a fact that Alpha Jack is scared shitless of me (most people are) and that's why he didn't try and attack me when I said anything.

I was brought back to reality when the yelling between the two became louder. Alpha Jack appeared to be extremely upset with his son for some reason unknown to me. His face scrunched with frustration as he jabbed his finger into his son's chest, then proceeding to part with a few final words. His son turned on his heels and returned to his seat, which, conveniently, was right across from me. I pulled my lips back and released a slight snarl as my canines extended from my gums. His disgusting scent hit me, but then just a fraction of a second later it oddly mixed with another more alluring one that I couldn't quite decipher.

My wolf began to stir in my head as I continued to take big breaths in. I was confused beyond belief. I could tell the strange scent didn't belong to the kid in front of me, which led me to believe that it was somebody he'd been hanging around earlier in the day or possibly even last night. My wolf's relentless whining finally got to me. I abruptly pushed my chair back, with enough force to push it over, and stalked out of the dining room. I shifted right when I reached the entrance of the building and darted off into the woods that surrounded that building. I ran for hours, only stopping once I realized it was growing increasingly darker, meaning I need to start getting ready for tonight. Why the hell did I say yes to Jarrod?

Once back in my confined room, I quickly showered to rinse off the sweat and dirt from my body before letting my shoulder lengthy wild hair air-dry like usual. I located the only pair of decently nice clothes I owned that I brought with me and put them on. I fiddled with the buttons on the black dress shirt for far longer than I should have, but with massive hands it's quite impossible to get the tiny buttons in their respective holes. I did a quick once over in the mirror, examining my matching dress pants and a black tie for wrinkles, not that I actually cared if I even had any. I was in the middle of putting my snug suite jacket on when my Alpha burst through the bedroom door. I growled at him for the intrusion, highly annoyed with him already because he'd forced me to participate in this ridiculous event. My growl was cut short when I saw his red-rimmed, puffy eyes.

He's been...crying?

The sight caught me off guard. I've never seen him cry. Hell, I don't think I've seen any Alpha cry in my 25 years of living. I immediately took a fighting stance, my body tense and waiting for instructions on who to kill. I wasn't at all prepared for what he did next.

Tipping his head back, he let out a loud, hearty laugh. My stance faltered as my eyes widened with surprise. I stumbled back, completely caught off guard by his actions. In the two and a half years I've known him, I've never heard him laugh.

"Calm down my boy, I have come bearing good news. Hell, not just good news. This is the best news I've received since my mate told me she was pregnant with my pups." He said while patting my shoulder in a fatherly way. I scrunched my brows and blinked a few times before nodded for him to continue.

"We have located our missing daughter. Alethia has been hanging out with her ever since we got here. Our little angel has been right underneath our nose this entire time. She's been living with Nightshade, those fucking cocksuckers. Listen, I will introduce you two later tonight, but for now this information needs to be kept highly confidential. I don't want Alpha Jack getting wind of our discovery. There has to be a reason behind their pack kidnapping her and keeping her for so long. I intend to get to the bottom of this, but for tonight we would just like to celebrate having our family all together once again." I tried to concentrate on his words as he spoke, but it became increasingly hard. The same scent that surrounded Alpha Jack's son earlier was now lingering on Jerrod as well, but it was much stronger this time. I couldn't help but take in a lungful of air. My wolf slammed against our barrier, and I could feel my eyes changing between my human side and wolf side.

"Xavier, are you alright?" He questioned, worry lacing his tone.

"Fine. Wolf and I ready to get night over." I curtly replied. Try as I might, I couldn't ignore Alpha Jerrod's sympathetic stare. It was burning holes into the side of my face. I growled under my breath, my only warning to him that I wanted to be left alone.

I knew what my chances were going into tonight's festivities. I was already 25; my chances were slim to none at this point. He cleared his throat and mentioned that we needed to get moving before we were late to our meeting place. We eventually made our way to the giant crowd of nervous males. I crossed my arms and leaned against the farther wall, observing my surroundings. Jerrod said his quick goodbye, explaining that he left his mate and girls in their room with strict instructions not to leave without him.

"They're going to murder me if I'm the reason they're late." He murmured nervously before practically sprinting away. The edges of my lips quivered with the possibility of a smile due to his eagerness to be with his family, but it stopped a moment later after realizing that what he's feeling now is the one thing I will never have the joy of experiencing. My mood turned even more sour, if that was even possible. My anger was tangible in the air and caused the large group of males closest to me to turn and watch me with fear in their eyes. I ignored them completely as I watched Alpha Jack stride into the room, his mate hanging on his arm.

Odd. All the Alpha and Luna's are supposed to be with accompanying the unmated females.

I shook the thought away and let myself admire how well this function was run. The council really did have everything planned out to a T. They kept all the males and females separate, with the entire group of mated Alpha's in the female wing with their mates to make sure that no male snuck into their wing and caused problems. They also made sure that the females were escorted to the building where the ball took place. I could understand the extreme precautions when it came to making sure someone didn't claim what wasn't theirs. A mate was the single most important thing to us male wolves. Nothing else in the world mattered to us once we found our other half. Well nothing else but the pups that she would soon bare. The need to be around your mate is stronger than anything else, only the scent of your mate or one of their belongings can curb the craving for their presence and attention. I couldn't stand being around my previous Beta, simply because his mate was never too far away. It made me feel even worse than I already did, knowing that I would never have that.

We finally reached our destination and I waited until everyone had already entered the now cramped building to finally make my presence known. People scurried to get out of my way as I walked, and didn't dare look me in the eyes. They already knew that I would be in a no bullshit mood tonight. Good. Within minutes the same scent that had been taunting me all day hit me with full force like a wall. My wolf forcibly broke the mental barrier I had put up between the two of us and took complete control of my mind.

He snarled, making me go rigid as I watched from the sidelines of my own body. It wasn't a snarl of anger, or annoyance. No, it was a snarl of pleasure. Delight. He growled at everyone around him, letting them know to get the fuck out of his way. He had his sights set on something across the room. Something that I had yet to navigate with my own eyes just yet.

When I did, my mouth went dry instantly. This can't be.

Chapter 7

X avier's POV

I couldn't formulate a coherent thought. My mate was here. She was actually fucking here. I had waited seven years for this very moment, seven of the longest years of my life. The last three of which the majority have been spent in my wolf form, all on my own. I didn't think twice about my wolf having taken all control. I knew for a fact that this was a fight with him that I wouldn't win, so surrendering all control without question was by far my best bet. Not to mention, he would be able to locate our mate faster than I could because of how many scents were lingering in the room at the moment.

This moment was monumental for my wolf. This right here was all he had. She was all he had. Obviously I had similar feelings towards my mate as he did, but after our family died he didn't take an attachment to anyone, whereas my skin side had taken a slight one to the Bloodlust pack. I sat back, almost as a bystander in my body, and vaguely observed the people around me as my wolf frantically searched the crowd, never ceasing his growls once. If this weren't such a serious moment, I would be the slightest bit amused at how they all cowered away from the power my wolf was currently radiating. Even the Alphas that were in my general vicinity grabbed their mates and fled to another region of the ballroom.

Some of the she wolves that were loitering around me had noticed the lust that was, without a doubt, swimming in my now black eyes due to the promise of our mate. They started to pathetically try and get my attention. They should have known it was a lost cause, but my wolf made sure to shut down their high hopes with an aggressive display of sharp teeth – he, as well as I, hated the wandering eyes that weren't our mate. I was easily disgusted by she-wolves that threw themselves onto those that weren't their mate. It was highly frowned upon amongst the werewolf community.

It made me proud to know that no woman, human or wolf, has ever had the pleasure of my body. The only woman who ever will, will be the one destined for me by the Goddess herself. It does shame me slightly to know that I used a few human females throughout my younger teen years for a meaningless blowjob here and there, but I've grown since then. It wasn't very hard to refrain from using a random female to get off when I needed it because most females were usually too afraid to ever approach me, but their fear was misplaced. I would never lay a hand on a single woman with the intent of doing physical harm; my mother raised me better than that.

With every passing second my wolf grew more and more agitated that he didn't already have our mate in his arms. We had strong Alpha blood in our veins, so it shouldn't have taken more than thirty seconds to find her, but her scent was muddled just the slightest bit by all the people in the room.

My wolf growled out in frustration. He was seconds away from tearing my hair out, when suddenly our eyes snapped to a semi-secluded area by the bar, all the way across the room. I pulled my wolf back, knowing that he would scare our mate with his intensity if I didn't take back at least a sliver of control, and I didn't need her to hesitate when it came to accepting our bond.

I began taking determined strides towards where I sensed my mate's presence. People parted like the red sea for me as I barreled through them, only one thing on my mind. An Alpha from one of the Northern packs made the mistake of trying to approach me. Clearly he has a death wish. I growled at him to back off while shooting daggers at him with my eyes; sending him a clear message to fuck off. I shoulder checked him as I shot past the idiot. Beginning to panic as I stopped to sniff her out again and it seemed like her scent had faded; that or someone was trying to mask it. Minutes ticked on with me just standing in place trying to sense her once again.

What if I don't find her before the end of the night?

At this point, nothing would be able to satisfy the hunger that had been stirred deep within my belly except for my mate.

Finally, as if the Goddess herself was looking down on me with mercy, a short yet thickly curved body with long blond curls cascading down the entirety of the back came into my line of sight. I knew it had to be her because of the way the wolf began to pound against our barrier once again, almost more intense than the time before, raging at me to go to her.

My chest tightened and my heart began to pound so hard that I could hear it's frantic beating in my ears. My hands itched with the basic, primitive need to touch her perfect voluptuous body all over, to cover her with our scent and ward off any other male that might look her way. My canines fully extended from my gums for the second time tonight, almost painful with the intensity that they descended with.

I was within about 50 feet of her when my eyes skirted to the male that was standing far too close for me and my wolf's liking. I was close enough now that she must have caught my scent and felt my presence. She jerked her head up and spun around so that she was now facing my general direction. We locked gazes seconds later and my breath caught in my throat.

Fuck, she's beautiful I thought to myself. My wolf purred obnoxiously in my head, pacing like crazy with need for her. If I were in wolf form, I would pounce on her.

Her big blue eyes widened while her jaw dropped. An unreadable expression flashed across her face before she stumbled backwards, clearly caught off guard. The slight movement had me fuming, but I couldn't fault her. I could never fault her. I knew it was because I looked ready to kill at any moment. Thanks to that fucking pup I grumbled to myself.

"MINE!" I roared. Everyone in the dining room went silent before all eyes were settled on us. I heard the shocked gasps and could feel the blatant stares from those around us. My age wasn't a secret amongst our community, so this was just as surprising for them as it was for myself that this was happening to me.

When I was finally within arms length of her, I reached out and grasped onto her incredibly wide hips, with little difficulty because of the thin gown she was wearing, and roughly jerked her into my embrace. I wrapped one arm tightly around her waist and threaded the other hand through her deliciously thick strands, pulling her impossibly closer and nuzzling my head into the side of her neck. I deeply inhaled her mouth-watering scent as a growl of pure pleasure escaped my lips. My cock twitched in my pants as her scent surrounded me, caressing every inch of my being in a warm, fuzzy embrace. If we weren't in a room surrounded by gawking bystanders, I would rip the silk material clean off of her just so I could get more of these enchanting sparks wherever our skin met.

My wolf's purring had become obnoxiously loud, but I didn't give a single fuck, quite frankly. I didn't have a fucking care in the world right now, as a matter of fact. It also didn't help that she had begun to rub circles into my chest with her palms that had been awkwardly crunched up against me because of our position. Not that I was complaining. Never.

She let out a content sigh and I couldn't help the smirk that made its way to my face. I affected my little mate just as much as she did me. The sound of someone impatiently clearing their throat brought my dreamland crashing down around me, much to my irritation. I let out a growl of annoyance, hoping whoever the hell dared to bother me and my mate during our intimate moment would get the hint to fuck off and leave us alone. Clearly it didn't work, because they cleared their throat a second time.

Somebody wants to fucking die today.

I reluctantly pulled my face an inch away from my mate's neck and glared at the little pup that was standing with her before.

"What?" I barked out, my words almost barely understandable due to my wolf's presence. I let my distaste for him known through my glaring eyes. I could tell that he was about to reply with some smartass comment, so I rose to my full height of 6'8 that had been cocooned around my beauty, tightening my hold around her waist and silently daring him to challenge me with his words.

I could see the regret instantly flood into his eyes. He opened and closed his mouth repeatedly, struggling to find the right words to say. Clearly, he sensed that I was in a "no bullshit" mood. I opened my own mouth to tell him to fuck off, but someone beat me to it.

"Leighton, it's fine. I am fine. You can go." My head snapped down to the beautiful girl in my arms so fast, I'm surprised I didn't give myself whiplash. Her voice caused a delicious shudder to run up my spine and I know she noticed by the way she was digging her teeth into her bottom lip to suppress a full-blown smirk. Her voice was just like I imagined it to be.

It wasn't soft and dainty, but full and held confidence that I couldn't help but find incredibly sexy. It had a slight rasp to it, and I knew that if I could only hear one thing for the rest of my life, it would be her voice speaking to me. I let my thoughts wander to how she would sound moaning my name while pounded into her relentlessly. I unintentionally let out an animalistic growl of want at the thought and ground my rock hard erection against her stomach. I watched amused as she flushed a deep crimson, knowing exactly where my thoughts had traveled.

Licking my lips, I thought about just how far that teasing little blush of hers went. Instead of waiting for the kid – whose name was apparently Leighton – to respond, I let my hands instinctively find my mate's ass and give a firm squeeze before returning them to the hips that were made just for my hands and turned her so that her chest was pressed fully up against mine once again.

I didn't waste a single second before beginning to attack her neck with open-mouthed kisses, not even bothering to care about who was standing around, ogling upon my possessive display of affection. My mate's dainty little hands clutched at my suit jacket as a quiet moan escaped her lips. Someone yet again cleared their throat and I pulled back, completely pissed off at this point. The only thing on my wolf and I's mind was pleasuring our mate until her voice was gone from excessively screaming my name over and over again.

"What now!" I yelled, searching for whoever had the balls to try and interrupt my mate and I. I met the amused, and maybe a little pissed off, gaze of my Alpha and I narrowed my eyes at him. I didn't give a shit about how disrespectful I was being to him right now, he knew how important this was to me.

"Xavier, I see you've met my daughter, Aceso." He growled out slightly, the edges of his lips quirking up in a shit-eating grin. My eyes widened as I peered down to my mate, who I now knew the name of. I felt my already immense love for her grow as she stared up at me in wonder.

"Wait, you're Xavier?" Aceso asked me incredulously. Her father cut me off before I could respond.

"I'm glad you two were bonded to each other, but if you ever grab my little girl's ass in front of me ever again Xavier, I will personally beat the shit out of you." My wolf forced himself forward, annoyed that someone was telling us where we were allowed to touch our mate, but I pushed him back. "Oh, and if you ever hurt her in any way, the same deal applies." He finished, giving me a stern look. This time, I didn't keep my wolf at bay. I was equally as pissed that he would even insinuate that my wolf or I could ever hurt our personal gift from The Moon.

I growled threateningly and took a menacing step towards Jerrod, but I was immediately tugged back.

"Please calm down." The voice of my sweet girl pleaded with me, which was then accompanied by the same soothing circles being rubbed upon my chest. My tense body relaxed and almost melted under Aceso's soothing touch. I nodded and kissed her temple before trailing my nose down her slim neck again, inhaling her addictive scent once more, leaving my wolf now completely at ease.

"Well I'll be fuckin' damned." I heard someone mutter in disbelief. I glanced up to meet Jerrod and his mate's amazed stare.

"What?" Aceso asked with genuine curiosity.

"No one has ever been able to calm him down when he gets into one of his moods. No one. Usually it takes hours for him to be okay around others and to calm his wolf down, but all it took you was three measly words." He shook his head and let out a disbelieving chuckle before pulling his own mate into a tight hold. Aceso let out the most adorable noise while yawning and I watched her nose scrunch up with adoration before she rested her head against my chest and cuddled into me. I chuckled lightly, the foreign noise sounding odd to even my own ears.

"Goodnight. We go to room now." I muttered out

"I don't fucking think so!" Jerrod fought back. I was about to voice my opinion, but Aceso's mother beat me to it.

"Oh, put a sock in it Jerrod! You were the exact same way after you found me, you damn hypocrite." She accused while giggling the last part, sounding oddly like her daughter.

"That's exactly what I'm worried about." He grumbled to himself. "Just keep your damn hands off of her while I'm around, you hear me?"

I didn't even bother to reply, rather just shrugging my shoulders before quickly dragging Aceso and myself away from the irritated Alpha. Aceso giggled at my antics the entire time and my heart began to beat a little bit faster at the sound.

Chapter 8

A ceso's POV

I tried my best to keep up with Xavier's large strides, but it was proving to be quite difficult due to the heels I was wearing. Eventually, we managed to slip out of the building through the back doors of the ballroom undetected. We weren't really breaking any set rules about not leaving the ball early, but it was highly "suggested" that all attendees stay until the very end of the event. Needless to say, it was a suggestion most newly found mates ignored.

Once we were outside, it became even more challenging to not fall behind. Xavier must have noticed my struggle, because he gently pulled me to a stop while chuckling at my expense. I puckered my lower lip out slightly in a fake pout, to which Xavier responded by bending down to my height and placing a chaste kiss to the puckered lip. He then proceeded to crouch down and pick up one of my heel-clad feet. My body swarmed with warmth from the simple touch against my lips and I reached up to run my fingers lightly over my still tingly flesh.

Quickly grabbing onto his insanely broad shoulders to keep myself from falling over, he began unbuckling both of my shoes before slipping them off. I moaned in relief. Why women ever wore those damn death contraptions was completely beyond me – they hurt like a freaking bitch.

He placed a delicate kiss to my ankle before gathering both of my shoes in one of his large hands and threading our fingers together with the other. I fixed my gaze on our entwined hands - completely enamored with just how big his hands really were when compared to my own dainty ones. They completely engulfed my much smaller hand. I was convinced that everything on this man was overly huge.

Though he was an incredibly intimidating size, I couldn't help but love how natural and right everything felt with him. He didn't scare me at all. In fact, I wanted nothing but to be surrounded by his warmth every single second for the rest of my life. My wolf's constant purring only seemed to intensify the longer I thought about Xavier. She's been doing it ever since we locked eyes earlier. Gauging by her reactive growls of pleasure, she had the same assessment of our mate as I did – he was one big hunk of sexy man.

I let my mind wander to how perfect today has been as Xavier led me to wherever we were going. In the matter of a couple of hours, I had been gifted with the perfect family, one that actually loved me, and the best mate I could've ever asked the Moon Goddess for. My heart swelled with happiness and I squeezed Xavier's hand in mine while also trying to ward off a fresh wave of happy tears. He glanced down at me with love swirling in his bright green eyes and began rubbing his thumb over my knuckles in a soothing gesture. I felt my adoration and bubble of love for him in my chest grow even bigger than it already was, if that was even possible. I felt like I was going to burst at the seams with happiness.

He adverted his gaze back to the gravel path ahead of us and I allowed myself to shameless check him out. I was suddenly hit with just how manly he really is. He easily towered over my 5'7 frame by more than a little. He had to be at least 6'7, if not taller, and his body consisted of pure muscle. His face was set with a now stoic expression and I could see why he probably instilled fear in most. His gaze was daunting and had I not been his mate, I would probably tuck tail and run off to hide. His nose was straight and he had the strongest jaw line I've ever seen. The way he squared his shoulders and managed to look so imposing made my nipples harden and my body to swarm with heat. My reaction embarrassed even myself.

I knew Xavier could smell my arousal because his nostrils flared and his grip on my hand tightened ever so slightly.

His husky growl was so loud that it vibrated against my body, causing me to gasp out in pleasure. The message it carried was plain and clear – want for his female. I sucked in a deep breath and tried to quell the heat between my legs while quickly fixing my gaze on my feet. My skin flushed bright red with evidence of my arousal and embarrassment.

I've never felt this...this needy for a single individual ever before. Xavier growled louder this time and swiftly picked me up bridal style, practically sprinting towards our destination. I giggled at his impatience to get us back to what I assumed would be his room. Although unnecessary due to his firm hold, I clutched onto his neck tighter, wanting to feel skin on my own.

Xavier's POV

I held onto my mate's little body for dear life as I maneuvered my way to my room as fast as I could without causing my angel any sort of dizziness. I tried to keep my animalistic desires under control, I really did, but it was so fucking hard when I was around Aceso. She was so naturally sexy it wasn't even funny. Her body was beyond perfect and it made my mind blank, every single thought just seemed to disappear except for my most carnal desires.

Her delectable blush made my nether region stir with need and I simply couldn't hold myself back any longer than I already had. It didn't help one bit knowing my innocent little beauty had been thinking the same thoughts that I had, either.

We finally managed to reach my bedroom door, which I forcefully kicked open, not giving a single shit whether I broke it or not. The only thing on my mind at this very moment was pleasuring and marking the gorgeous women in my arms. I turned and immediately dropped Aceso, pinning her to the door we had just come through. I grabbed the skirt of her dress and ripped it in half, effectively getting it out of my way.

"Xavier! This isn't my dress!" Her sweet voice scolded me while slapping her dainty hand against my chest.

"Don't care. Need to touch you." I muttered out before shoving my knee in between her newly uncovered thighs and moved them apart, making room for myself between them.

I lifted her body up against my own, trapping her between my large frame and the door behind her. She grew quiet, seemingly shocked by hearing my voice for only the second time. I looked up, meeting her eyes as we intensely stared at each other, our faces so close that our noses were brushing against one another.

I didn't waste another second before smashing my lips upon her rosy pink ones. A throaty moan erupted from Aceso's chest, awakening every fiber of my being and sending my body into overdrive. I needed to hear that absolutely erotic sound again. I began moving my lips feverishly against her own, slightly surprised that she had managed to keep up with my punishing pace. She eased her fingers into my hair and tugged, eliciting a wanton moan from my own lips.

Darting my tongue out, I ran it along the seam of her plush lips, begging for entrance. She quickly denied me access, which had me playfully growling at her. I moved my hands up her thighs and harshly grabbed one of her plump ass cheeks within my hand and squeezing. The action caused her to gasp in surprise. I took advantage of the moment and shoved my tongue into her mouth, moaning at how sweet she tasted. We massaged our tongues against one another as they fought for dominance. My body nearly became numb with the intense pleasure coursing through it.

I reluctantly pulled away from her now swollen lips and ripped the front of her dress the rest of the way open with my claws, pulling the now shredded clothing away from her body and uncaringly throwing it on the ground. I let my eyes greedily wander over her underwear-clad figure, unable to stop the loud growl of approval from escaping my chest. She flushed a deep scarlet color and began to squirm in my arms, clearly uncomfortable with being so exposed in front of me.

"Wait! Wait. I'm not ready to... um, mate just yet. I'd like to get to know you a bit better first. If that's okay..." She whispered, trailing off towards the end. She grinned at me sheepishly while resting her hands against my chest.

I knew for a fact that she was a virgin - that much was obvious due to her 100% pure scent. I nodded my head in response, letting her know that I had heard her request and was willing to comply. In that moment, I knew that I would do anything this perfect beauty asked of me. I was 100% completely whipped already and it hasn't even been a full two hours since I've met her. Taking a few deep breaths, I tried to calm myself, as well as my wolf, down from the powerful moment we had just shared with our mate. It was of no use, though.

"Need mark you. Please." I begged her, still trying to regulate my labored breathing, which was proving to be very difficult with the smell of her arousal still suffocating me. It was moments like these that made my choppy English an issue.

Instead of answering me, she pulled her hair to one side of her body, completely baring her neck to me. I moaned out from her obvious display of acceptance and submission. Latching my mouth onto her jaw, I began trailing open-mouth kisses up and down her neck until I reached the pristine flesh between her shoulder and neck.

I nibble and sucked harder on the sensitive area of skin, drawing out an endless stream of moans from Aceso. Not being able to hold my wolf back any longer, my canines extended and I swiftly sank them deep into her creamy flesh. She released a scream of pain that was almost instantly replaced by a crazed moan of pleasure.

I retracted my teeth and licked away the blood that had trickled out, prompting the wound to heal rapidly. Her curvy body sagged against my own as she rested her head as close to the crook of my neck as she could. Her breathing began to slow as the after effects of the marking continued to drain all of her energy.

I noticed that she was too tired to even keep her eyes open, so I walked her over to the bed, cradling her against my chest as I went. I gently laid her down as she whimpered from the loss of my soothing touch. She sat up in bed, searching for me. I smiled softly before pushing her back down and stroking her cheek with my thumb to calm her sudden unease.

Right here. Just changing. Promise." I rasped out. She let out a relieved sign before falling back onto the plush pillow that I had used the night prior. I threw my suit jacket off and began unbuttoning my dress shirt, all the while my eyes never left the woman curled up under the sheets of my bed. I couldn't wipe the cheesy smile off my face even if I tried. She was absolutely perfect in every way. The seven-year wait for my sleeping princess was, without a doubt, worth it. I would wait until my very last breath for her, and even longer if I had to.

I pushed the love filled thoughts aside and climbed into bed, wrapping my arms around Aceso's waist before pulling her flush against my chest. I cocooned my body around her own, engulfing her small body with my warmth completely. She turned in my arms and snuggled impossibly closer. Pressing a kiss to her forehead, I allowed myself to drift off into the best night of sleep I've ever gotten, filled with promising dreams of my own Luna and I's future.

Chapter 9

A ceso's POV

I'd been drifting in and out of consciousness for about half an hour now, not wanting to wake up and face the rest of the world just yet. There'd been a heavy weight resting upon my chest ever since I first stirred this morning, and from the tingly sensation that was accompanying the dead weight, I knew it was, in fact, Xavier's massive body resting atop mine.

I eventually pried my eyes open and glanced down, only to have my heart melt at the sight in front of me. Xavier had his entire body covering my smaller frame. His head was using my chest as a pillow while one arm was wrapped securely around my waist and the other was gripping my thigh. He had effectively ceased any movement I could possibly make because his legs were also tangled amongst my own. In other words, I was totally and utterly caged in. The position made me giggle at how possessive and protective he was – even in his damn sleep.

I took this as an opportunity to memorize his features and engrain them in my brain. He looked completely at peace. The dark circles that lingered under his piercing green eyes were no longer present, and he the frown lines due to his constant scowl Alethia had told me about earlier were gone. He looked at least five years younger and even more handsome than before.

Dear Goddess, this man is going to be the death of me...

I ignored the fact that he was basically crushing me under his massive weight, because this moment was far to perfect to ruin for something as miniscule as breathing. I let my eyes wander over his short obsidian locks, unable to resist the temptation of running my fingers through them any longer. They were even softer than I imagined them to be. It was like I was handling pure silk. Xavier instinctively leaned into my touch, seeking the comfort that only I, as his mate, could provide him.

Suddenly, a loud purr echoed through the room. The abrupt noise slightly scared me, causing me to jump lightly in shock. I tried my best to hold in my laughter at the ridiculously loud noises of pleasure that were uncontrollably radiating from his chest. I had no doubt that his wolf was responsible for the commotion.

I couldn't hold back the laughter that had bubbled up in my chest any longer. The giggle, although rather quiet and breathy, still caused Xavier to stir from his deep slumber. I watched quietly as he - much to my displeasure - unwrapped his arms from around me and pushed himself ever so slightly onto his elbows, examining me in his delirious/half asleep state. He inhaled deeply before repositioning himself so that his head was tucked directly into the crook of my neck, letting out a loud sigh as soon as his body rested against my own once again. He released a content hum as he continuously breathed my scent in and out. I could tell that he had already begun to let sleep pull him under again, and let out a loud laugh in response. The movement from my laugh jostled his head, causing him to groan out in annoyance.

"No." His deep voice rumbled, sending vibrations throughout my entire chest. I nearly moaned at how husky and sexy his voice sounded in the morning. It was definitely a sound I could get used to.

His words registered in my head and I scrunched my eyebrows in confusion. "No?" I asked.

"No." He growled again before shushing me and attempting to fall back asleep.

"What do you mean "no"?" I asked again before continuing to run my fingers through his hair, slightly digging at his scalp with my sharp nails. He groaned deeply at the action.

"Want sleep. More." He said, trying his best to form coherent sentences.

"But I want more of you." I pouted, hoping he understood that I wanted to keep talking and get to know him, though I was completely oblivious to what I had just insinuated at.

Before I even had time to process what was happening, Xavier had removed his body from its position on top of me and had thrust my legs apart, occupying the space between them with his big burly frame just like he had last night. His hands roamed the planes of my body, heating my body up even more than it already was from the heat he generated. Gripping my thighs tightly, he rubbed circles into the flesh that was just mere inches from my now-throbbing core. He leaned over, pushing every inch of his scorching body against my own practically naked one in a whole new way. He licked a strip of skin from my collarbone to my ear, nibbling and pulling on it harshly once he reached my mark. I moaned loudly as my hips unconsciously jutted up, grinding against Xavier's rock hard length that was now straining painfully against his boxers. He released a ferocious growl that was dripping with need – just like the reaction It had on my body.

"Smell so good. Want you now." He declared between his assaults on the sensitive skin covering my neck. I audibly gulped as I tried my hardest to rein in my hormones and cool myself off, but I was failing miserable. If I didn't get away from him right now I was going to jump his bones over and over again.

"P-pee. I have... to pee." I forced my words out through clenched teeth, hoping desperately he and his wolf would cooperate with me. He let out a displeased huff and moved just enough so I could squeeze out from underneath him and dash to the safety of the ensuite bathroom. I snatched his discarded dress shirt off of the floor on my way before slamming the door behind me. I turned and rested my head against the dark wood while trying once again to calm my labored breathing and rapidly beating heart. I turned on the faucet and splashed my face with cold water, which did little help to cool me down.

I wasn't sure how long I stood in the bathroom doing breathing exercises that I always practiced with the she-wolves that were in labor. Slipping my arms through the dark fabric in my hands, I pulled it on quickly before bringing the shirt up to my nose and inhaling Xavier's enticing scent greedily. I was lost in my own little world until I felt two strong arms coil around my body from behind.

I looked up with the intention of examining Xavier once again, but I stopped dead in my tracks at my very own appearance. My jaw dropped as I feverishly examined the huge, purple hickies that covered the majority of my upper neck and chest area. I could feel Xavier's penetrating gaze burning holes in me as I reached up and brushed my fingers over the beautiful mark that now marred my skin.

I gasped at the simple contact, which caused my legs to grow weak and give out. Xavier clutched me closer to his body as he began to place light pecks all over my discolored skin surrounding his mark. When he finally reached the newly scarred skin, he left a hot, open-mouthed kiss directly upon it that caused my body to go completely slack in his hold while my insides turned to jelly.

He sniffed me before releasing a pleased growl and stating, "Smell like me. No male come near now. Mine." I knew the last part was his wolf speaking, and I'd be damned if it didn't turn me on once again. I blushed profusely when I felt his thing poking me in the back.

Shit.

"Want to mate you. Need to mate you." He whispered right next to my ear.

"Uh-huh." I moaned out without thinking. Every last bit of his jade eyes were engulfed into the black pits of his wolf. In mere seconds, I was once again pinned to our bed with Xavier hovering closely above me. He began trailing kisses down my neck to my stomach and then right above the waistband of my all lace panties. I was a moaning mess at this point, unable to formulate a single coherent thought even if I wanted to.

Before I could stop him (as if I even wanted to), Xavier had ripped the undergarment away from my body and pinned my hips to the bed. I wriggled in his hold, feeling considerably uncomfortable with my most intimate parts on display right in front of his face. Not to mention so up close and personal.

He licked his lips and spoke, "All mine, yeah?" I gulped and nodded in response, my arousal so thick in the air even I could smell it. I was about to pull away from his probing gaze until he began sucking and biting at my inner thighs, working his way towards my now dripping center. He was relentlessly teasing me and my frustration was rising to unbelievable heights.

"Dammit, Xavier, please!" I whined between shallow pants. I don't know how much more of this amazing torture I could take.

"What you want? Tell me." He replied, his warm breath blowing against my oversensitive skin. I whined once again, exasperated and needing release.

"I-I don't know. Please Xavier! I just, I need..." I trailed off, unable to finish my sentence. Without warning, Xavier licked a hot strip up the center of my core, latching his mouth onto my throbbing bundle of nerves and sucking harshly. I screamed out in surprised pleasure as I fisted the sheets securely in my palms. I tugged against the expensive Egyptian cotton until it ripped within my hold from how hard I was pulling. I roamed my hands over the bed, searching for something to anchor me to reality as Xavier wrecked havoc on my weeping pussy. I gave up and threaded my hands through his hair, the same way I had done this morning – although this was for an entirely different reason. I would've laughed if I weren't in such a compromising position.

Xavier clasped his large hands under my knees and pushed my legs up towards my chest before thrusting his tongue into my heat. I arched my back up off the bed and fought back the urge to cry because of the intense pleasure he was giving me. The new angle allowed him to pleasure me so much deeper than before, and with nothing but his skilled tongue. The thought of how he became so good at this should have bothered me, but he was my mate and my mate currently had his head between my thighs, eating my pussy like it's the last thing he'll ever do – so I let the thought slide for now.

I didn't think the pleasure could get any better, but that was before he glided one of his long and thick fingers into me, pumping it in and out slowly while still nipping at my clit and continuing to hold my legs up in the same position with one strong arm. He eased a second finger in, stretching my walls deliciously.

The feeling of ecstasy from him working me over and the slurping of him roughly sucking while his fingers pounded in and out brought me to the brink of my high, and It took only mere seconds until I was clenching around his digits and hoarsely yelling out his name.

He slowly eased his movements to a stop, pulling away from me to lean his body against the back of his calves while my legs came to rest on either side of him. He scanned me from head to toe, and I knew without a doubt that I looked thoroughly satisfied...for the time being.

I gazed back at Xavier through hooded eyes and watched as he smirked at me while his eyes sparkled with pride. He reached up and wiped my slickness off of his mouth and chin with the back of his hand. As wrong as it sounds, the action was incredibly sexy and I found myself licking my lips.

"Taste so good." He half moaned half growled.

"Mmmmhm" Was all I could unintelligibly mutter out. He chuckled quietly to himself while attempting to rub his calloused hands all over my body once again, only to have me swat him away with each time.

"Nuh-uh, I'm hungry. Unless you found a way to magically turn yourself into a big plate of pancakes and bacon, then you can take yourself, and your grabby hands, and get me something to wear from my room." I stated before fluttering my lashes at him.

"Don't want my sausage?" He said, faking confusion. My eyes widened and I chocked on my spit, which resulted in a mini cough attack due to his sexual innuendo. He chuckled loudly before removing himself from the bed and carelessly throwing some clothes on.

"My queen, I be back with clothes." He announced before shutting and locking the bedroom door behind him. My heart melted at his nickname for me. Though, I guess what they said about alphas and being overprotective when it came to their mates was most definitely true.

Sighing loudly, I slid out of bed. My weak legs quivered as if it were my first time walking. Once I finally felt confident enough that I wouldn't collapse after a few steps, I slowly made my way to the shower. I rinsed off, letting the scalding hot water massage my muscles. By the time I had stepped out of the shower, there was a clean pair of black leggings and one of Xavier's sweatshirts sitting on the counter for me.

He knows me so well I thought to myself as I examined my beloved yoga pants. I ignored the fact that he picked out the most racy set of lingerie I had packed and slipped the articles of clothing on before wandering out into our bedroom. I silently reveled in how Xavier's sweatshirt drowned my physique before his amused chuckle brought me out of my reverie. I blushed lightly at him catching me in the act, but forgot about it quickly once my stomach rumbled loudly.

My nerves began to build with every step we took closer to the dining room. All male and female wolves would be joined together once again because everyone that was left on the island was now with his or her mate. Unmated males and females who hadn't found their other half during the ball had taken a plane off the island late last night. Or so Xavier had managed to tell me. He began rubbing his thumb over my knuckles, soothing away any tension that had built up from my slight freak out a few minutes ago. I smiled up at him lovingly and pecked his cheek before we entered the dining hall.

The second we stepped over the threshold of the imposing French double doors, all eyes were on us. I seized up, hating the fact that I was the center of attention.

"Calm down, they stop staring eventually." Xavier's warm breath whispered against my ear. I nodded before hugging my body closer to his side, seeking the protection that he gladly gave me. Snaking his arm around my waist, he kissed my forehead before leading us towards a large dining table in the center of the room that my parents were currently sat at.

Xavier pulled out the chair to my father's left and sat down before grabbing me and situating me on his lap. I burrowed my face in the crook of his neck to hide my developing blush due to the intimate position he'd put us in. Not to mention, in front of an entire crowd of people. Loud rumbles of laughter could be heard from the other Alpha and Luna's that were occupying the seats around us. I was saved from further embarrassment when one of the servers scurried over to take our food order.

"Go ahead. Get whatever you want." Xavier sweetly murmured in my ear. I smiled, finally hearing a full sentence from him.

"Can I have three pancakes with scrambled eggs and bacon? And a cup of apple juice to drink, please?" I asked sweetly, knowing how shitty it was to have to wait on others. I'd had my fair share of doing that in my old pack whenever an important dinner was being held. The girl smiled and nodded before turning her gaze to Xavier, but not actually making direct eye contact with him. I saw him glance at me with a devilish smirk adoring his face from my peripheral vision.

Uh oh. Nothing good can come from this...

"No. I already ate." He said before winking at me as he finished his sentence. I gasped as my stomach dropped to my ass. I CANNOT believe he just said that in front of everyone! In front of my fucking parents!

"Xavier!" I squealed at him while slapping his chest. He just laughed along with everyone else as they clearly caught on to what he was insinuating. I leaned my elbows on the table and hid my face in my hands while everyone around me continued to laugh at my expense. Well, everyone except my father - who was glaring menacingly at Xavier. I'm glad they found this funny because I was going to fucking murder him when we were alone. My embarrassment was quickly squandered and replaced with fiery anger.

"I don't know why you're laughing, you're not getting anything from me after that shit you just pulled." I hissed at him matter-of-factly. Xavier's smile instantly fell and his eyes widened as he processed my statement. His helplessness only made the roaring laughter grow louder around us as he tried miserably to beg for my forgiveness with frustrated broken sentences and whimpers. My father's grumbles turned into whole-hearted laughs.

I smiled triumphantly and crossed my arms in front of my chest, leaning back against Xavier's hard chest once again. I refused to give into his endless pleas for forgiveness. I'll let him sweat this one out for a little while. That'll teach his stupid ass.

Alpha Jack's POV

I silently made my way into the dining room, making sure not to attract any unwanted attention to myself. My anger spiked once I saw whom Leighton was referring to when speaking about about Aceso finding her true mate at the ball.

I thought he was just lying to me and going behind my back so he could be with that piece of shit, powerless mate of his. He hadn't quite gotten the grasp of how important his mating with Aceso was. Sure, it may possibly weaken her incredibly powerful wolf to be mated to someone who wasn't her true mate, and yes it might kill her true mate in the process, but I didn't really fucking care. The only thing I cared about was being back on top of the food chain. Those fucking Bloodlust scum had stolen that position from us decades ago, and I was determined to be the leader who put us back on top.

Aceso was the key to our success, and after eighteen years of smooth sailing, I refused to announce defeat now. We were so close to the end goal, I could almost taste it.

My agitation grew when I realized it would be much harder to steal her back now that her I knew her true mate was the fucking Xavier Campbell. I wouldn't be in this damn forsaken situation if my son had just followed the fucking simple instructions I had given him. It really wasn't that hard: stick with Aceso, wait until the room goes chaotic with males grabbing and claiming their respective mates, drug her, and then snatch her out the back door before she finds her own mate or vice versa. Leighton was an alpha for fuck sake! He should've been able to stand up to that Wild piece of shit and finish the only job he had been assigned.

I reached up and began rubbing at my temples, trying to get the massive headache I've had ever since yesterday night to go away. I growled when I felt my mate's hands try to rub soothing circles on my back. I just needed to be alone right now so I could figure out where the hell I was going to go from here.

At least it didn't appear that her father and mother had figured out that she was their daughter. I had the lingering affects of her suppressants that I'd ordered Donna and Ray to feed her since she turned 10 to thank for that. I knew with due time they would wear off and begin to raise questions as well as noses. I could only pray that I managed to do some hush hush damage control before shit hit the fan. I forced myself to calm down as I reassured myself that my father and I's hard work would pay off. The intricate plan we concocted years ago was fool proof. We couldn't fail.

Yes, but you never planned on losing that damn she wolf either! I thought to myself. My wolf growled in frustration and snapped his jaws at me.

As if I didn't already have enough problems right now, now I have a pissed off wolf to deal with too. Being around so many Alphas in one small location was starting to get to him.

I abruptly stood, ripping my mate, Cynthia, up from her seat as well before storming out of the dining hall. I ordered her to hurry up and pack her shit. She tried questioning me, but I thankfully got her to shut her mouth with the help of my Alpha command. We left quickly, boarding our last minute plane back home to hopefully formulate a plan of attack. Linking my father, I told him we would be home early and to have a meeting with the elders ready by the time I got back.

Chapter 10

A ceso's POV

I still wasn't ready to forgive Xavier for being such a bonehead at breakfast, so I decided a suitable punishment would be the silent treatment. No male ever wanted to experience their mate intentionally ignoring them. It was complete torture not only for their wolf side, but also their human side as well. Most male wolves craved their mate's attention constantly - It was all they really cared about - so you can imagine how it made them feel when they are deliberately snubbed by the one person they want the most.

Xavier and I had retiredd back to our bedroom after breakfast to spend some "quality time" together. Little did he know of my plan to get back at him, but he caught on quickly. Once he realized the full extent of what I was doing, he panicked.

"Aceso? Promise I never do again. What do you want? Rub your feet? You said they hurt from shoes. I run you a warm bath? Watch movie? Please? Talk to me." He begged. My resolve was quickly withering down to practically nothing at all and I knew I would have to give in within the next few minutes. Hearing him try to string together sentences was my ultimate undoing. I know he's not used to talking, that much I gathered from his past as being a Wild, but here he was trying to negotiate with me. I turned away from him and headed towards the balcony doors when I heard the most heart-shattering whine resonate throughout the room. It caused a pang in my chest that I couldn't ignore. I quickly turned back around to face him, unable to stay "mad" any longer.

I sighed before saying, "If I ever catch you pulling some shit like that ever again, we won't be sharing the same bed until I decide you've earned the privilege back. Understand? What we do in the bedroom is for us to know and no one else." He quickly nodded his head up and down eating up the space between us in three large strides and enveloping me into his huge, muscly arms. His warmth soothed my wolf and I instantly, doing away with any guilt we previously had over causing him any emotional distress.

"Does still count if somebody else bring up? You're little loud, my queen." He teased cheekily. My cheeks heated up ever so slightly and I groaned before pushing at his chest. He took the hint to shut up before pulling away from me and latching his plump lips onto my own.

The kiss we shared was full of raw passion that had my knees quivering, barely able to hold my own weight up. At that moment, I couldn't remember why I was ever angry with him in the first place, but I did know I would never get used to his kisses. They were all consuming and made my toes curl with bliss every single time. I broke the kiss first; needing to breathe and regain what little sanity I had left.

"We need to stop, Xavier. The plane is leaving soon and we haven't even started to pack." I spoke breathlessly. He was clearly unhappy with my statement because he began to pout like a five-year-old child.

"Don't wanna pack. Wanna keep kissin' you." He grumbled, trying to persuade me with his best puppy dog eyes that he could muster. I had to fight back the laugh that threatened to escape because of the sight before me. Xavier, who was a grown man, was actually pouting because he wasn't getting his way. Unbelievable.

I quickly looked away from him and focused my gaze on the beach through our room window. I knew if I stared at him any longer, any ounce of self-control I had would be completely thrown out the window and I would end up letting my mate have his dirty way with me. I know that I made the right decision in deciding to wait until we were back in the safety of his – our – pack before mating, where I knew no one would bother us, but it was times like this, last night, and even this morning where I was beginning to second guess myself. It was taking so much more effort than I originally thought it ever would to keep myself from jumping him every two seconds.

Damn you hormones!

I could wait. I know I could. The moment would be perfect. We would be in our pack house, in our very own room, on our very own bed, with nothing separating our bodies. Perfect. The memory of Xavier's calloused hands roaming over my bare body this morning caused goose bumps to arise rapidly. We needed to get home, and quickly.

"You know Xavier, the faster we get packed, the faster we get home, the sooner you get to bury yourself in me and officially make me yours. So, we can either stand here and kiss or we ca-" I didn't even get to finish my sentence before he was frantically running around the room, shoving all of our things back into random suitcases with renewed vigor. The sight itself was enough to have me in stitches.

I rested my head against the small plane window, my mind blank of all thoughts as Xavier absentmindedly drew patterns on my legging covered thigh. The action was making me sleepy, but I didn't mind. I wasn't too keen when it came to flying. Ever since I saw the Grey's Anatomy episode where they were all stranded after their crash, I'd become much fonder of long car rides instead.

The flight was going just fine, but I suddenly became very uncomfortable. The longer Xavier's hand rested on me, the hotter I became. I could feel the burning heat from his touch intensify and it was almost as if there wasn't a single barrier between his skin on my own. All of a sudden, an agonizing pain rushed to my head, and I gripped my skull between my hands. I applied mild pressure, hoping to get the abrupt headache to go away, but it was no use.

Xavier sensed my obvious distress and tried to sooth me, but nothing was working. My internal body heat seemed to kick up another notch and I was finding it hard to breath. It felt as if my body was cooking itself from the inside out. As another wave of pain attacked my head, Xavier's hold on my thigh tightened to the point of bruising me.

"Fuck." He hissed through clenched teeth. I glanced over at him to see his eyes completely black and clouded with lust and want. He shut his eyes and sucked in a deep breath, trying to reign in his wolf. I could see the tent in his pants gradually growing despite his effort to make it stop. When he finally opened his eyes again, they were darker than I've ever seen them and I knew then and there that he had lost all control over his human side to his wolf. This wasn't going to end well at all.

"Aceso." He growled out. His voice was so deliciously deep and husky it caused the searing pain coursing through my entire being to flare once again, only more intense this time. I let out a sharp squeak as he ripped me from my seat and firmly planted me onto his lap, jutting his hips upwards while simultaneously pushing my hips down, effectively grinding his already rock hard length against my soaking wet core. I let out a feral moan, and silently thanked my lucky stars that everyone around us was either asleep or had headphones in, and that we were hidden away from all the other passenger's view from our seats in the back corner of first class.

"Aceso." He growled out again, but this time his voice was even deeper and more demanding. The sound alone was enough to have me grinding my hips against him once again. I couldn't believe this was happening now of all times. Couldn't my stupid fucking body have just waited another two damn hours for the plane to land before it threw me into heat? Why of all places did this have to happen on a fucking airplane where people were surrounding us - two of which just so happened to be my parents who are currently seated three rows ahead of us.

"I can't – we have – you're in" Xavier couldn't formulate a single coherent thought as every fiber of my being was screaming with need for him. That was the point of heat. Its sole purpose was to give a marked, but not yet fully mated, couple the final push they needed to lose all control and finish what fate had intended for them. This meant intertwining their DNA together and becoming one. It threw a female's body and hormones into complete and utter overdrive until you and your mate couldn't take it anymore. The pain and need for the intimate touch of your other half became unbearable. Most couples didn't wait long enough before fully mating after marking for heat to even take affect.

Although I was thankful that Xavier understood my want to wait, I couldn't help but mentally curse myself out as the pain refused to let up. I'd read all about heat for my biology class. Every article said that the pain wasn't supposed to take effect until after about an hour of it beginning, but it's been barely five minutes and I'm failing to fight off tears. They also said that just the simple touch of your mate's skin upon your own would be enough to dull the side affects until you finally decided to consummate your bond, but if anything, Xavier's touch was only making things worse.

As the minutes ticked by, my strength dwindled and my tears had begun to flow freely. Xavier wasn't providing me any comfort either; he was too preoccupied trying to hold his wolf, who refused to give control back, from mating me right here, right now. I could see that it was breaking him to have to witness me in so much pain and not be able to do anything about it. Well, there was something he could do, but I had no intentions of joining the mile high club – as of right now at least. I can't guarantee my answer will be the same in another 30 minutes.

My cries of pain gradually raised in volume, until they couldn't be ignored anymore. If there had been any unmated males on this plane, they would have known the second my heat began. The scent of an unmated female's heat is the second most enticing smell to a male wolf, right after the scent of his mate.

My parents were the first passengers to notice my obvious distress. My mom immediately realized what was happening and sprang into action. Jumping from her seat as if someone had lit a fire under her ass, she came charging towards me. Xavier was quick to notice her swift incoming, and flipped our position so that his body was in front of mine, caging me into the seat. He released a terrifying growl before baring his elongated canines at her while extending his claws. Everybody quickly got his message of "come close to my mate and you die".

My mom looked helpless. She knew there was nothing she could possibly do to calm Xavier down while I was in this condition. My shriek of pain promptly got his full attention back on me. He picked me up and cradled me in his arms as he tried to sooth the burn by kissing my skin anywhere he could reach. Black dots began to cloud my vision and I knew there wasn't a damn thing I could do to keep myself conscious. Not that I really wanted to anyway. I gladly gave into the darkness, letting it consume me along with the mind-numbing pain I was in.

I wasn't sure when my next episode of heat would take place. It could be five minutes from now or five hours from now. I prayed to the Moon Goddess for the latter because I knew I wouldn't be able to handle anything close to that type of pain any time soon.

My body jostled mercilessly wherever I was. I wanted to scream at whoever was near me to cut the shit out, but my voice had evaded me. My mouth was dry and my tongue felt like sandpaper. I tried to swallow, which proved to be much more difficult, as well as painful, than it should have been. I mustered up every last ounce of strength that I could and cracked my eyes open. I was met with darkness, except for a weird bluish-green glow from in front of me. Someone gently push the sweat-coated hair from my forehead, and by the mildly irritating tingles they left in their wake, I knew it was Xavier.

"How you feel?" He asked, his voice barely above a whisper. Before answering, I examined his eyes, taking notice that he was once again back in control, assuring me that my heat was gone - for now at least. I couldn't find any energy to try and speak or even mind link a response to his question, so I let out an exhausted sigh/whine instead. He seemed to get the hint as he leaned over and pecked my forehead, dropping the topic.

It took me a few minutes until I realized that I was in the back of a car with my head resting on Xavier's lap. I was assuming we were on some sort of gravel road because of how bumpy the ride was. Xavier's strong arms wrapped around me and pulled me into a semi leaning position with all of my body weight resting against his chest. I lulled my extremely heavy head back to rest on his shoulder, unable to keep it upright on my own.

"Don't know how long until next heat wave. Lucky it hasn't come yet. Don't understand why touch isn't helping, but I don't think I can hold back next time it hits." He whispered worriedly in my ear. I nodded in reply, understanding what he meant. There was going to be no holding off our mating until we got to know each other, that much I knew.

Right after he finished his sentence, white-hot pain surged through my body, causing me to cry out to no one in particular. With the condition my body was already in, I knew that if Xavier and I didn't finish what we started last night, I wouldn't live to see tomorrow. Xavier began to panic behind me and started growling frantically at the driver in the front seat.

"Alpha, we're still an hour and forty-five minutes away from the border of our territory. I'm already going thirty over the speed limit. There's nothing more I can do." The driver rushed out nervously. Xavier let out a frustrated growl before punching some button on the ceiling of the car. I heard a strange whoosh noise and was vaguely aware of the partition that now separated us from the rest of the car. Before I could even think, Xavier had shoved his hand into my pants and began to pleasure me with his thick fingers. I sucked in a large breath of air and spread my legs farther apart for him, thankful for the slight relief in pain he was providing me. I could only hope his distraction tactic worked until we reached our territory. I couldn't imagine having my first time in the back seat of a car, but then again I wasn't sure what how far my heat could push my limits.

Chapter 11

Xavier's POV

I did my best to distract Aceso from the torture she was experiencing with my fingers, but I knew that there was only one thing that would cease the pain all together. I sucked on her mark harder when she dug her nails into the skin of my wrist out of discomfort. My fingers only provided a tiny release for her for about five minutes before she began to cry from the agony once again. It was tearing me apart to know that I was the cause, and the solution, to her current predicament. Dear Goddess, I wanted to wait until she was ready to mate because that's the only thing she's asked of me, but my wolf and I were suffering just as much as she was from simply watching her try to endure this.

I pulled my fingers from her dripping heat and made quick work of shedding her of my sweatshirt and her leggings. As much as her exposed skin would tempt me, she was sweating profusely and it was making the situation worse than it already was. Deep sobs began to rack her body as her heat got worse. My vision grew blurry with my own unshed tears of helplessness.

"X-Xavier I c-can't do this a-anymore. I need...I n-need-" She cut herself off with her own ear-piercing scream as she dug her nails into the leather seat, clawing the material open in the process. I already knew what she was asking for before she even started her sentence. She'd finally caved and couldn't take the pain any longer. I didn't expect her to, but I was absolutely beside myself.

A huge part of me was ready to give my mate what she needed and put her out of her misery, but an even bigger part of me knew that when she finally came to and was in a sound mindset, she was going to regret the decision. I was at a crossroads with myself when her hand jerked back and clutched my family jewels in a death grip. Her pain seemed to subside long enough for her to clearly voice her request, or rather threat, to me.

"If you don't put an end to this mother fucking heat right now, I will cut your balls off and put them in a display case on the goddamn fireplace." She hissed out between clenched teeth. My eyes bugged out of my head as she tightened her grip when I hesitated. I groaned out before ripping my shirt off of my body and lifting her hips so I could lay it under her. She's already fucked up the upholstery of the car, but I knew she would be even more embarrassed if she left a bloodstain too.

I hurriedly removed all of my clothes before ripping her remaining underwear off and reclining the seats all the way back. I was attempting to make this as comfortable as possible for her. I prayed to the Goddess that Beta Aaron would drive safely, since neither one of us had a seatbelt on at this point.

I resituated her body so that I was kneeling between her legs before reaching down to play with her swollen clit, making sure that she was thoroughly wet so there was as little resistance as possible. I wasn't by any means small - at all, really - and I knew from this morning that she was incredibly tight, so it would be difficult for her to fit me at first.

"Look at me." I demanded. I knew she was about out of it, and I hated bossing her around like this, but I needed to warn her so she was prepared. That and I needed the final push to know that what we were about to do was really what she wanted at this moment in time. She struggled to meet my gaze, but when she did she let her eyes wander down to my achingly hard manhood. Her jaw dropped and her body tensed.

"How the fuck am I supposed to fit that gigantic thing in me!?" She hysterically yelled. I refrained from laughing at her comment and put my hand under her chin, forcing her eyes back to my own.

"Its okay. Stretched you a little this morning and you're already wet. Going to hurt a little bit, but I promise it'll feel good soon, yeah?" I cooed. Dammit, this whole "sucking dick with words" thing is beginning to become a problem. I'm going to have to spend more time in my skin form so we can communicate better with time.

I started running the tip of my dick up and down her slick folds, lubing myself up with her juices. I gave her clit extra attention before spreading her legs as wide as they could possibly go and pressing the tip of my member into her tight heat. I had to hold back from blowing my load then and there because of how fucking good she felt. I was barely inside of her and my head was already swimming. I eased into her heat a few inches at a time before I finally nudged up against her hymen.

Deciding to go with the old "rip the band aid off" method, I pushed the rest of the way into her with one quick thrust. I heard a sharp intake of breath before she threw her head back and released a loud, animalistic moan. Arching her chest up into me, she thrust her perky breast into my face. Stilling for a moment, I wanted to give her a chance to get used to the feeling of me filling her completely before continuing.

"For the love of everything that is good and holy, please move." She begged me, her voice raspy and thick with need. I released a desire filled growl before pulling all the way out and thrusting back in, more powerful than the first time. She wrapped her legs around my waist and sunk her nails into my back as we began to move together at a deep and fleeting pace. She soon met my every thrust and the pleasure was becoming almost too much to handle. The only sounds that could be heard were the slapping of our skin against one another and her never ending moans as I sucked on her sweat-slick skin. I gripped her waist hard enough to bruise as I was pounding into her mercilessly. She clawed at my back so hard I could feel little droplets of blood cascade down my back, but it only turned me on more. She whimpered as her climax began to approach so I released one of my hands and began to rub little circles into her clit all the while still stretching her walls with my cock. Seconds later, she hit her high and exploded, coming all over my length as I continued plunging into her, drawing out her earth-shattering orgasm. She milked me into my own release and I shot thick beads of my seed into her while I buried my face into her neck. I sank my teeth into her mark, officially making her mine as our DNA wove together.

I retracted my teeth as my body slumped against her own, trying to regain control of my ragged breathing while my mind recuperated from the intense high I just experienced.

I finally pulled out, leaning back far enough to examine Aceso and make sure she was okay. Her eyes were closed and her breathing had slowed down slightly and evened out, assuring me that she was fast asleep.

I reached over and cracked the back windows open just enough to let the crisp January air cool the both of us off, as well as to hopefully get rid of the heavy scent of sex that lingered. I gently pulled the seats back into a sitting position and re-buckled Aceso in, not wanting to risk her safety any longer. I didn't realize how much time had passed until Beta Aaron started knocking on the partition to let me know that we had finally arrived at the pack house.

I slipped my sweatpants back on before redressing Aceso in her slightly damp pants, deciding against the heavy sweatshirt.

Clear out all unmated males from the property. Get them as far away from us as possible. Wolf is on edge and will lose his shit if male looks at our mate I said to Beta Aaron through our pack link. I managed to retrieve one of my many black shirts from one of the suitcase in the back of the trunk before slipping it over Aceso's bare body, careful not to jostle her around too much and wake her. I heard someone's footsteps approaching the car and let out a menacing growl of warning.

Another step and you dead I spat to whomever the on-coming footsteps belonged to. A throaty chuckle met my ears before I picked up the sound of retreating footsteps and allowed myself to relax slightly. I stepped out of the car, never removing my eyes from Aceso for even a millisecond. Reaching over and cradling her against my chest, I let my warmth surround her body so that she didn't get too cold from the nippy winter air.

The second I turned around I was met with Alpha Jerrod's intimidating glare. He'd obviously picked up my scent and realized that it was now intertwined with his daughter's. That paired with her evident lack of clothing, and he was definitely passed the point of being pissed off. I watched as his mate tried to calm him - though it wasn't working at all.

"You've got about three seconds to explain to me exactly what went on in the backseat of that fucking car, boy." He spat at me, animosity written all over his face.

"Didn't have a choice." I growled out, annoyed with his accusing tone. "I either mate her or watch her die slow, agonizing death. I think we both agree I made right decision. " I retorted back. To think that I would intentionally give my mate, and his daughter, anything less than the world made my wolf and I both seethe with anger.

I watched as his jaw clenched in anger before he stormed off into the pack house. It would definitely take the both of us a day or two to cool off from our...disagreement. I switched my gaze back to Aceso's mother who was still standing in front of me, and despite her husbands obvious displeasure with the situation, she had a knowing smirk on her face. I furrowed my brows in confusion at her reaction to the situation.

"He'll come around, you just need to give him a little while. He knows first hand how us Nightly women are a very hard bunch to resist. We know exactly what to say to get our way. It seems as if my little girl here is no different." She cackled at the end of her speech before shooting me a wink and spinning on her heels to follow after her own mate. I shook my head at her retreating back before making my way to my bedroom – one I'd hardly used since receiving it - and setting my queen down on our bed. My wolf purred loudly at the thought of falling asleep next to our better half every single night for the rest of our lives.

I threw open my suitcase in search of a pair of boxers to wear to bed when I froze. Resting on top of all of my belongings was a shiny gold box of condoms. Every male received his very own package when we arrived at The Island because the council knew how horny newly mated couples could get.

I picked the taunting little box up with shaky fingers as worry-filled thoughts rushed around in my head. I had no doubt in my mind that Aceso was probably pregnant now.

Not only did my family have incredible genes, but Aceso was also in her heat to top it all off.

This was bad.

This was very, very bad. We still had yet to figure out the reason behind Aceso's kidnapping, and I'll be damned if I put not only my mate, but also our first born, in harms way. Not to mention, if she wasn't ready to mate then she sure as hell wasn't ready to have my children.

My children.

The thought of Aceso walking around with a huge swollen belly while she carried our perfect creation made my heart skip a beat inside my chest. Fuck, I don't think I've ever wanted something more in my entire life. This was definitely something we were going to have to discuss, and soon. There was a chance, very slim, but still plausible, that she wasn't actually pregnant so I could be getting myself worked up for no reason. The only way we would know for sure is if we got the pack doctor to test her in a week or two.

Deciding to push the anxious thoughts off to a later date, I chose to forget all about the boxers I'd been searching for and just sleep naked. It's not like it's nothing my little minx of a mate hasn't already seen. Crawling into bed, I pulled Aceso into me once I was settled so that we were spooning. I was caught off guard when she unexpectedly swung her leg over and forced me onto my back, effectively straddling me. Our sexes were dangerously close and my member hardened instantly.

"What are you doing? Need to lye down, get some rest. You've been through lot today." I chastised as she began to rub her sexy little body all over mine.

"Too worked up to sleep. Need you again." She mumbled before attaching her lips to mine. If I had any self-control, I would have pulled her off of me and demand that she rest, but I was a weak man when it came to denying my woman what she wanted. We continued to lose ourselves in each other until the dark night sky peaked with light and we were both utterly spent, unable to continue for another second.

Aceso's POV

I finally gave into the heavy pull of consciousness as sleep began to escape me. Releasing a hefty sigh, I tried to roll onto my side on the bed. Key word here: tried. My every muscle screamed with agony from over exertion. I didn't even know it was possible to be sore in so many places at one single point in time.

I slid my hand across the mattress in hopes of it colliding with Xavier's heated body, but I came up short. I took a few deep breaths as I tried reining in my raging emotions – which were threatening to start up the water works – due to the lack of Xavier's presence. I forced myself to calm down and focus on the fact that his side of the bed was still very warm, meaning he had just recently left and his scent still lingered thickly in the air. Still, it didn't stop me from being slightly miffed that he hadn't woken me up to tell me where he was going or even mention that he was leaving me. I'm not usually clingy, so I knew this was all because of our freshly completed bond.

I finally cracked my eyes open all the way, blinking a few times to clear the haze out of them before I could actually make out the numbers displayed on the alarm clock. I giggled to myself in disbelief that I actually managed to sleep in until four o'clock in the afternoon. I've wasted practically my whole day away in bed. No wonder Xavier had to leave, he probably had a lot of shit he had to do today with him being the pack's trainer and all.

A flitter near Xavier's pillow caught my attention, and I quickly leaned over and snatched the measly little paper that was folded in half. I grunted in pain as I pushed myself into a sitting position with my back resting against the headboard. I unfolded the note and began to read.

"My Queen,

I didn't want to leave you this morning. Believe me when I say it is one of the hardest things I've had to do. There were some pressing issues that I couldn't ignore any longer. I didn't have the heart to wake you from your much needed slumber.

There are three guards patrolling the perimeter of the pack house as well as two of our best warriors right outside your door. I'm just down the hall if you need me, but I'm hoping to be back before you wake.

I love you. xx

-    Xavier"

I couldn't resist the urge to roll my eyes at his overprotective precautions, though I knew there was nothing I was going to be able to do to change it. Besides, if it weren't him then it would've most definitely been my dad.

I let out a content hum before wrapping the black silk bed sheets around my very naked body and slowly throwing my legs over the side of the bed. I then proceeded to hop down from the abnormally high bedframe, but the second my feet made contact with the floor my knees buckled and I crumbled to the ground. Grimacing in pain, I tried to move and make an attempt to get up, but I was stuck; completely paralyzed from the pain. I began to panic and was about to mind link Xavier for help, but he crashed through the door before I could even open our link. He must have sensed my distress and came to check on me.

My wolf purred out her satisfaction with our mate, content to sit back and let him take care of us.

"What's wrong? Why you on the floor!" He demanded, taking a few large strides towards my fallen body and scooping me up into his arms. He began to scan me head to toe, clearly looking for any injuries. When he realized that there was no immediate threat to my health, he took in what I was wearing - or more so the lack thereof. His eyes darkened immediately and I knew what was coming next if I didn't put a stop to it. I snapped my fingers in his face a few times before he finally looked at my face.

"Hey, hey, hey. None of that shit." I stated pointing an accusing finger in his face. "That's why I'm in this situation in the first place. I can't really...uh...walk on my own at the moment." I rushed out, looking away sheepishly. His booming laughter filled the room as a loving smile made its way onto my face. That foreign sound was something I could definitely get used to.

"Fucked you that good, yeah?" He questioned cockily. I flushed bright red at his bluntness while trying to push him away from me, thought he was having none of it as he pulled me closer. He began trailing his nose up and down my skin in the crook of my neck.

"Come my queen, let's take hot bath. That sound good?" He asked while quirking his eyebrow in question. I nodded my head quickly. If there were only one thing I was allowed to do for the rest of my life, it would be taking hot baths. Well, that and Xavier.

He filled the tub with a generous amount of honey and milk bath suds before he lowered me into the scalding hot water. He was worried it would be too hot for me, but I quickly shut him up with a pointed look. He slipped into the bath behind me before cradling my body against his own. We just sat there and talked. We talked about anything and everything. We talked about his childhood as well as his parents. He told me the entire story of his old pack and why he came to have the reputation that he does today while I rubbed soothing circles into his arms – which were wound tightly around me. I was fighting back tears at what my mate had already been through in the small time that he'd been alive.

"So, do you want to continue to beat around bush about what happened in back seat of Beta car or should we talk about it?"

There it is I thought to myself.

Xavier's voice had a playful undertone to it and I knew he was trying to make this conversation as stress free as possible for my sake, which I was very thankful for.

"I guess we should discuss that, shouldn't we?" I muttered softly. "I'm sorry for putting you in that position. I know it isn't what either one of us wanted, but what's done is done and there's no going back and changing the past now." I spoke calmly. This must not have been the reaction Xavier had predicted because he was silent for a couple of minutes.

"Oh...you took better than I thought would. You much calmer about this than your father, that for sure." He chuckled under his breath. I tensed considerably at his words.

"Shit! I didn't even think about how my father would react! What a wonderful first impression I've made." I grumbled, disappointed with myself. I can't even imagine what my real dad possibly thinks of me now. He probably assumed I'm just some regular hussy.

"No. Stop. He don't think bad of you, but I guarantee he going to want to chop my balls off next time he see me touch you." I giggled at his horrified expression, mainly because I knew he was 100% correct just from the short period of time that I'd gotten to know my father in. "I was thinking-"

"Well that's never good." I cut him off sarcastically. He pinched my side teasingly at the comment, causing me to squeal loudly.

"As I was saying." He said, sending me a playful glare. "Us getting married is inevitable. We already fully mated and commit to each other for life, so even though marriage is for human aspect, I think it make your dad feel better about the situation." I nodded in reply, glad that he was being so thoughtful and taking my family's opinions and feelings into consideration.

"I think that's a great idea. I can see it now." I said, looking up to the ceiling wistfully. "Us sitting on a swing that's hung up on our house's wrap around porch, watching our kids run around and play together in the yard." He tensed slightly at my mentioning of kids, but it was gone as soon as it came. I let it slide, but made a mental note to ask him about it later.

"How many kids?" He asked quietly.

"I don't know. How many do you want?" I asked back. I'd never thought this far ahead in life. I never saw a reason to until I met Xavier.

"Many as you'll give me." He stated seriously. I tucked my head into his neck and chuckled. I leaned back the slightest bit and got a glimpse at the determined look on his face before splashing him with the soapy bath water.

"However many we have, I'm sure it will be a dandy ole' time to tell them all about how their mother lost her virginity in the back seat of a car."

"Escalade, not car. Escalade more fancy. Makes it sound better." He teased, placing a chaste kiss against my cheek.

Chapter 12

A ceso's POV

Xavier and I made our way to the pack house's kitchen hand in hand after our soothing bath. It was still a little painful to walk due to the soreness between my legs, but I didn't dare say anything. Xavier's impossibly big ego didn't need yet another boost. The quiet roar of conversation quickly died down as we entered the room and I quickly adverted my gaze to the floor, hiding my nervously flushed face behind my curtain of hair. Xavier swiped his thumb across my knuckles in a soothing gesture before pulling me in closer to his comforting embrace. My heart surged with happiness as our eyes connected and I lost myself within his deep green orbs. The sound of multiple shocked gasps pulled me out of my trance and I waited for someone to explain what had happened.

"Aceso, your hair! It's like...glowing?" My father's confused voice spoke out. I furrowed my brows in confusion and reached up to touch my long locks. I glanced at them for a few moments before scanning the room, only to see that everyone else was sporting a similar confused and shocked expression. My father's eyes glazed over, so I knew he must have been mind linking the pack doctor or someone similar. Once he was done, he focused a much harsher gaze upon Xavier and crossed his arms, his jaw clenching and unclenching the entire time. I was about to speak out in my mate's defense, but I was swiftly cut off.

"Oh my god!" Spoke a low, breathy voice. I looked over to see who it belonged to and met the eyes of a short elderly woman. By the wrinkles that adorned her face and the aura of wisdom that emanated around her, I knew for a fact that she was a very highly respected pack elder. She had a slight hunch to her shoulders, but other than that - and her wrinkles - I could see no other signs of physical aging. She had bright, snow-white hair that was pulled back into a tight ballerina-esque bun. The corners of my mouth turned up in a slight smile when I saw that she was barefoot, just like me.

"What is it, Elder Esmeralda?" My mother inquired. The woman opened her mouth to speak but was abruptly cut off by my sister's squeal as she ran into the room. She rushed over to me and shielded her body with my own, earning her a possessive growl from my very unhappy mate. I didn't even bother to stifle the loud giggle that broke free from my chest at Alethia's ridiculous antics.

I followed her gaze to the large open hallway that led into the kitchen, watching as a huge muscular man shot into the room. He strangely resembled Xavier's enormous structure, although he was an inch or two shorter. His hair was a deep mahogany brown, and his iris's were a shocking silver hue with a hazel ring around the pupil. He also shared the similar deep tan skin as my mate, which I was assuming came from training outside more often than not. By his matured facial features I guessed he was probably twenty-two or twenty-three.

The man smiled wickedly before darting across the room, heading in Alethia and my direction. He didn't make it very far before Xavier charged at him, apparently sensing that he was a threat to me. For an alpha, he was being quite stupid. Anyone with a brain could obviously tell this man was Alethia's mate because of the loving glint in his eyes. Well, that and the mark that resided upon my sister's neck. He clearly was of no threat to me, but I'd like to see someone try telling that to my Xavier. The two huge brooding bodies collided against each other and Xavier made quick work of capturing the guy in a tight headlock.

"Calm down, cousin! I wasn't after your woman!" The other guy, who I now knew was related to Xavier, chuckled out. His voice was slightly strained from the pressure Xavier was exerting on his neck. It made complete sense to me now as to why the two men shared so many physical similarities. Xavier only grunted in response to his comment before finally releasing him from his choking hold. I went to step away from Alethia when she yelled again before gripping the back of my shirt to keep me in place.

"No! Don't! He's gonna attack me again!" She playfully pleaded.

"Babe, you started the tickle fight in the first place. I'm just finishing what you started." The man, who I had yet to be introduced to, said between bouts of laughter. I couldn't help my own adoring smile from creeping onto my face. They were absolutely perfect for each other and I could already tell he made her happy beyond belief.

"So are you going to continue to selfishly use me to protect yourself, or are you going to introduce me?" I cheekily questioned as I craned my neck to the side so I could look at Alethia while I spoke.

She cleared her throat before ever so slightly stepping out and to the side from behind me and saying, "Cece, this is my mate Rory. Rory, this is my twin sister Aceso." I saw a look of bewilderment appear upon Rory's face as he looked back and forth between the two of us, clearly trying to figure out if Alethia was just pulling his leg.

"Fraternal." We both stated at the same time. His perplexed expression quickly changed into one of realization and he nodded. Without wasting another second, Rory whizzed forward and captured Alethia is his arms before beginning to mercilessly tickle her sides. I giggled before I felt myself being pulled back into Xavier's hard chest. I could tell that he was still a little miffed at Alethia's actions through our bond, so I rubbed my hand up and down his arms that were securely wrapped around my waist in a soothing manner. Once Rory finally gave into Alethia's pleads to stop, I refocused my attention back on her.

"So, how did you two meet? And when?" I questioned while I watched in amusement as Rory held her like Xavier was currently holding me before he started to run his nose along the crook of her neck. Those two really are related.

"Well, first you have to know a little background info. Rory is Xavier's cousin, and was one of the only twelve that survived their pack's attack. Since he and Xavier were both born to be leaders, my dad put them in charge of all of our warriors. After you were taken, dad went crazy protective and I was basically never let out of my room. Had he given me more freedom, I probably would've met Rory right after he joined our pack. Anyway, after you two disappeared to do God knows what, my dad demanded Rory come and watch after me just in case anything were to happen. Both of us were pleasantly surprised and I guess the rest is history." She said, finishing her little speech.

"Hey! Just you both wait until you have children. Maybe then you'll understand the crippling need to protect your family and make sure they are happy and out of danger at all times." Our dad grumbled from across the kitchen. Alethia and I laughed at his words.

"Speaking of which, how are you feeling Sweetie? You looked like hell last night." My mother asked me.

"Gee thanks mom, but don't worry. We, um... took care of the situation." I said, cringing at how awkward it was to vaguely talking about Xavier and I's sex life with my parents. My dad let out a low warning growl as my mother cackled loudly at my obvious discomfort. The moment was cut short when my stomach growled loudly.

"I guess that's our queue that it's time to eat!" My mother exclaimed and dragged my father to the table while he complained under his breath. Everybody in the kitchen sat around the large dining table as we began to pile our plates high with food, Elder Esmeralda's earlier concerns completely forgotten.

Xavier's POV

I walked through the compound, monitoring all the male wolves as they sparred with someone of their same strength. I was just about to call out and begin a new training exercise when Alpha Jarred called out my name.

"Can I have a word with you?" He asked, looking a little nervous. I was instantly alert, afraid that there was something wrong with Aceso or there was an update on the Nightshade situation.

I followed closely behind him to his office after telling the men to continue training until I returned.

"Please, have a seat Xavier." He mumbled out before rounding his desk and plopping down into the worn down desk chair.

"What this about?" I rumbled out, wanting to get to the bottom of whatever was making him skittish quickly.

"There's something I've wanted to ask you for a while now, and the events that occurred at the ball this weekend only solidified my decision. As you know, my wife and I had a hard time conceiving the twins, and we were never able to have another kid. We don't have a male to pass my title down to and it's high time that I retire. My mate and I discussed this with great care for the past few months, and we've decided that you're our best option for the Alpha title. With you being Aceso's mate, it just strengths my belief that you should be the one to take my place." He finished, looking 100% sure of himself.

"What about Rory? He could lead." I questioned. I wasn't too keen on leading a pack again. Not after what happened the last time...

"We did consider it quite a while ago, but he's not serious enough. He's a little selfish as well, and an Alpha has to be willing to put the pack before anything else. He couldn't do that. Plus, I still need someone to train my warriors when you hopefully take over."

"I won't put pack before mate. Never. If you want me to, then answer is no." I growled out.

"I don't expect you to put the pack before your mate, no Alpha ever does. So...what do you say?" He said, searching my face for any give away to what my answer will be. I didn't respond right away, giving myself a few minutes to mull over what he was asking of me.

I sighed deeply before saying, "I guess. When do I start?" His eyes lit up at my words and he sprung up from him chair.

"You'll start today. There's a mound of new member paperwork that needs to be done and I figure that will get you into the swing of things. This is wonderful! My mate will be so pleased to hear the news." He said before rushing out of the office. I rolled my eyes before getting up and making my way to the Alpha office, mind-linking Rory on the way that he would be in charge of training for the rest of the day.

I shuffled through the gigantic mound of paperwork that sat tauntingly on the desk. I switched back and forth between signing paperwork and then scanning it through to the computer system to document it electronically - just in case something was to happen to the hard copies.

The entire process took longer than normal, but it was something I was used to doing ever since my father first started training me to become my pack's Alpha. Our meticulous attention to detail and thorough documenting was why our pack was always run so well. The only thing we really lacked was harsh training techniques because my father didn't see the importance, which ultimately led to our downfall. That was why I was so harsh on Bloodlust's warriors. Never again would I be a victim to another greedy pack.

Although there was a significantly larger amount of wolves in this pack compared to my old one, I couldn't help but notice that it was much easier to handle the heavy workload. I knew without a doubt that it was because I now had my very own mate. Before, when my father would assign me the daunting task of drawing up new treaties or trading propositions to be sent to another pack, I would dread every minute of it. I would rather get my teeth pulled without being numbed than do the paperwork. My father used to tell me that what I was feeling was common, that it had to do with our wolf being caged in and taking on the responsibility of an entire pack without someone to assist me. But now, I found myself working at a faster and more efficient pace so that I could get back to holding Aceso in my arms and run my hands over her silky smooth. Make her purr in content... fuck.

I was almost finished with all the necessary paper work concerning pack member transfers, due to the mate's ball as well as the new pups that were born over the weekend, when Aceso walked into my office. Her scent instantly flooded the office and calmed my wolf. She made her way to me before sitting on the armrest of my swivel chair and resting her hands, one of top of the other, on my shoulder. I leaned back in my chair and stared up at her lovingly while caressing her thigh gently. She supported her chin on her hands and pecked my temple before standing back up.

She moved around to the back of my chair and stood on her tiptoes while trying to reach my shoulders. I watched in amusement as she let out a frustrated huff when she still couldn't reach. I chuckled lightly when she walked around the chair to stand in front of me once again, this time sporting an adorable pout.

My laugh instantly halted when she climbed up onto my lap, straddling my thighs, and began to knead my shoulders in her hands. I groaned before letting my head fall forward to rest in the crook of her neck while she massaged at my tight knots. Pride surged through our bond and I knew that both Aceso and her wolf were very happy that they were able to make me feel good - so good.

Aceso giggled like a little schoolgirl causing me to look up, perplexed as to what she found so funny. I raised one eyebrow in question. She removed her fingers from my shoulders before crossing her arms in front of her chest. It took every ounce of self-control I had not to glance down at her voluptuous chest.

"I knew my massages were good, but I didn't think they were worthy of a standing ovation." She said, smirking triumphantly before glancing downwards. I followed her gaze and felt my cheeks lightly heat up when I realized exactly what she was talking about.

She reached underneath the Henley I was wearing and scratched her nails down my stomach, causing me to release a deep, needy moan. I threaded my hands in her hair before pulling her head forward and crashing my lips upon hers, to which she responded immediately. I thrust my tongue in her mouth and moaned at her sweet taste. She suddenly ground her hips against my now pulsing length and I swore I was going to explode from the sensation. I clenched her hips in my hands and rubbed her against my groin once again, except more forceful than she originally had. The action had us both whimpering desperately. I began sucking harshly on her mark as she fumbled with my belt, hastily trying to get it undone. We were so wrapped up within each other's touch that we hadn't realized the door to the office had been opened.

"Jesus, can you two keep your hands off of each other for more than two minutes?" I heard Aaron huff irritably. Both our eyes shot up to see Beta Aaron standing next to Jerrod while about five of our pack warriors lingered behind them. Aceso gasped loudly before making a move to crawl off of my lap, but I wasn't having any of it. When she realized I wasn't going to let her up, she slapped her hands over here eyes and hid her bright red face in my chest.

"Would it fucking kill you to knock?" I growled out, extremely irritated that my intimate moment with my mate was ruined.

"Would it kill you to save such actives for the bedroom?" Aaron retorted back with a sarcastic snort.

"Hey! This is my daughter we're talking about! Watch it!" Jerrod growled, his penetrating gaze switching between both Aaron and I. Aceso mumbled something along the lines of 'kill me now' into my chest which caused us all to laugh.

"We're here to discuss Aceso's kidnapping. It's actually quite convenient that she's already here because most of the questions we have about those Nightshade bastards are for her." I nodded and picked Aceso up and shifted her on my lap so that she was leaning against my chest and could participate in the conversation.

"Sweetie, can you tell me about the time you spent in their pack? Everything you tell us could be helpful in some way." Her father spoke encouragingly. She nodded and cleared her throat before speaking.

"They never treated me very good. Everyone truly believed that I was a low-rank omega. I was never allowed to play with the other kids when I was little because they said I was too weak and that I would just end up getting hurt and being more of a liability to the pack. I was also never allowed to leave and go on the school field trips to other packs. They always would make up dumb excuses and punishments for things I never did to keep me on pack grounds. When I was about twelve was when they said I needed to start pulling my weight and doing my share around the pack. I would be required to clean the main rooms of the pack house everyday after school. I had to make sure all the dishes were done and put away, wipe away any dust that had collected, and I was expected to vacuum too.

It wasn't until I turned fifteen that they began demanding that I start working at the pack daycare on top of it all. I hardly ever had a single moment to myself between all of that as well as homework. I never had any friends except for one of the warrior's daughters, Elizabeth." She finished speaking and I could feel myself shaking with rage. To say I was pissed was an understatement. The way that piece of shit pack treated my mate was unforgivable. They treated her like she was their fucking personal maid. No omega, or anybody for that matter, deserved to be treated like they were nothing. She whispered soothing words into my ears and the tremors began to subside.

"We had the pack doctor's test your blood you gave earlier. She said there were large amounts of suppressants present in your bloodstream. I have no doubt that they were feeding them to you so that nobody would question your omega status. They must have been wearing off during the ball though, because although your power wasn't heavy, it wasn't weak enough to be an omega." Her father explained.

"Oh!" She suddenly yelled out, catching everybody's immediate attention. "There is something else! Like I said, I never really had friends, but I was really close with the Alpha's son. His name was Leighton. He'd hang around me all the time when I was cleaning the house and we quickly became friends. He was the only higher rank that actually treated me like a human being. The week of the ball he started to act really weird. He told me that him and his dad got into an argument because he wanted to escort me to the ball and the Alpha didn't want him to, but then that same night my parents, sorry fake parents, tried to tell me that it wasn't their fault I had to go with Leighton and that it was Alpha's orders." Everyone in the room got similar looks of confusion.

"I don't understand why either of them would lie about the situation, but that does seem really fishy. There has to be something going on between the Alpha and his son. Exactly what it is, I don't know, but I'm going to get down to the bottom of it. Until then, Beta Aaron and I have come up with a plan we think might just work.

With you taking over as new Alpha, we're going to have you contact Alpha Jack with a request to go over a new border contract. We are going to try and lure him here, but I don't think he's dumb enough to fall for that. We'll set the meeting up for three months from now so that we have time to train, because we plan to capture that bastard of an Alpha and torture him for answers." Jerrod finished his sentence with a sneer. It wasn't the best plan I'd heard, but it was all we had. There was no way to find out why they'd taken Aceso other than to talk to the man behind the crime himself.

Chapter 13

A lethia's POV

I rolled my eyes as my dad's eyes glazed over. He was obviously mind linking for someone to come and babysit me since Xavier was out of the picture as of five minutes ago. I knew he didn't have it in him to keep him from my sister while forcing him to stay here and watch over the both of us. Not that Xavier would have even listened, anyway.

We were all shocked, to say the least, when Xavier not only found his mate, but it ended up being my long lost sister of all people. What a small fucking world, huh?

"I've informed Rory of the situation and he's on his way." My father's calmer voice spoke. I could tell he was less freaked out now.

"Fantastic." I muttered, not bothering to hide my annoyance with him. He sent me his famous I-know-I'm-being-a-pain-in-the-ass-but-you-have-to-deal-with-it glare. I blew out a puff of air through my lips before continuing to scan the humongous crowd of people. I thanked my lucky stars that I was a werewolf because it took a lot to make us sweat and it was really hot in here. I couldn't imagine my mate seeing me pitting out in my dress. The image itself made me giggle.

I didn't say anything further in protest because, really, I'd heard he was a fine piece of man and I didn't mind ogling at him all night. Well, until he or I found our mate that is. It's considered very disrespectful to flirt or pursue someone that isn't rightfully yours, especially if they have found their mate. Suddenly, I heard someone clear their throat, catching both my father and I's attention.

"Sir." The man said bowing his head at my father. I was totally and one hundred percent frozen. My fucking mate had been living in my pack this whole fucking time and I never even knew it! He then adverted his gaze from my father to me and it took less than three seconds before the most beautiful thousand-watt smile lit up his face. My dad looked slightly confused until I threw myself at him and wrapped my arms tightly around his neck.

"What the fuck is going on here? Have you two been seeing each other behind my back?" My father asked with a hint of anger in his voice. I didn't respond as I was far too occupied in my mate's presence. He had the most amazing eyes I'd ever seen and I knew I would forever be getting lost in them.

"Answer me!" My father boomed, getting more irritated by the minute.

"Jarrod, you dumbass! They're mates!" My mother scolded while slapping him upside the head. I didn't bat and eye, as I was in my own little world.

He cradled my cheek in his hand and rubbed his thumb across my cheekbones, leaving a trail of fiery tingles in its wake. My eyes fluttered closed on their own as I took in a deep breath, moaning lightly when my mate's enticing smell registered in my nose. It was the most intoxicating thing I'd ever smelt in my entire life. He grasped my intricate hair up-do in a tight grip before thrusting my head to one side, revealing my perfectly unscarred skin. He licked and sucked on my neck before, getting my hormones even more worked up then they already were.

His canines extended before I even knew what was happening and harshly bit down, marking me as his. My eyes shot open in surprise. Why, I have no idea. I knew this was coming and there was absolutely no doubt in my mind that this was what I had wanted. I think it was just the initial pain that caught me off guard, well that and the fact that my father was still, for some reason unknown to me, watching our interaction.

I slumped my body against my mate's larger and more solid frame as I saw my mother drag my father away from us in my peripheral vision. He put up quite a protest, but she shut him up with one look.

"Time to go. Now." I heard Rory growl against my ear, his hot breath fanning across my ear and neck. I involuntarily shivered as I felt the telltale poke right on my stomach before giggling like a little school girl as he swiftly threw me over his shoulder and made a beeline for the exit.

Chapter 14

Aceso's POV

It's been about three weeks since I arrived at my new pack. With everything that's taken place it my life, this has got to be some of the most uneventful few weeks I've ever experienced. Xavier has been hovering over me 24/7 and I'm going slightly crazy – not from his company, but from how overbearing he is being. I can't do anything by myself, and ever since I helped him better his speaking, all he does is protests and demands that I let him do everything for me. Well, that and talk dirty to me, but that was the one thing I did enjoy...a lot.

I don't know if the behavior is because of the fact that our mating didn't go as either of us had planned, or the fact that he's been waiting so long to finally find me. We've already talked out and discussed our feelings on the touchy subject that was how we consummated our bond, and Lord do I know that he feels bad - I do too for putting him in that position - but seriously! It's not like there's a glass box around my emotions! And to make matters worse, every time I call him out on his antics, he does anything and everything in his power to change the subject. It's absolutely infuriating.

I pushed the annoying thoughts aside as I heard Rory yell out to get everyone in the clearing's attention. I glanced around the training field and took note of how built everyone in this pack was. There wasn't a single person who was out of shape, including all the women. That was the other thing that made me incredibly proud of Xavier. In almost every pack I've ever heard of, the Alpha will refuse to let any of their women train. They said it was because their wolves would be distracted from fighting and they would ultimately get hurt. When I asked Xavier for his input on the subject when I realized this pack was different, he said that although their wolves would be anxious about their mate fighting, it was also better to know that your mate could hold his or her own during a fight if push came to shove. He also told me that Jarrod was extremely against the whole idea when he first came to the pack, but he soon came to change his mind after Xavier incessantly prodded him about it.

His reasoning and his ability to make change was just another reason why I knew Xavier was an amazing Alpha. I believed that as an Alpha, you aren't just born into your title. It needs to be earned. You should gain the respect of your people and you should be experienced enough to make wise decisions that are ultimately going to affect a large group of people later on. Xavier had that. He thought things through, and used logic both logic as well as instinct to make a sound decision, instead of ruling off of just pure emotion, like a lot of Alphas tended to do.

Stepping up to the gym mat that had been laid out, I waited for Xavier to show up. Yes - he let me train - but ONLY if it was with him. Figures. He pouted for thirty minutes about it when I said he should be focusing on his Alpha duties instead. Men.

"Sorry I'm late baby, got caught up talking with some men about border patrols." Xavier's deep voice rumbled out behind me. I shrugged my shoulders to let him know that I didn't care about his lack of attendance before leaning up on my tiptoes and pecking his cheek. He started to ramble on about what he was going to be teaching me today, half of which I didn't catch because I had dosed off. I'd been really tired as of lately and I wasn't quite sure why.

"Aceso, are you even listening to me?" He asked while narrowing his eyes. I shot him a sheepish look before shaking my head. He let out a frustrated huff while crossing his arms. He then proceeded to retell me everything he had just said, much to his chagrin. We got halfway through, and I could tell he was holding back the entire time we were sparing. I let it slide in the beginning, thinking he might step it up the longer we sparred, but he didn't and it was beginning to piss me off.

"God dammit, Xavier! Stop going easy on me! Do you think some random wolf is going to hold back just because I'm a woman? No!" I yelled at him, letting my temper get the best of me. I could tell his wolf really didn't like the way I was speaking to him by the way his eyes began to swirl and darken.

"You will not be fighting ever. Do you understand? This is just precaution. You're lucky I'm even letting you train!" He shot back, gaining the attention of almost everyone in the clearing. My blood began to boil as my anger shot through the roof. I was one of our best fighters already. Matter of fact, he told me that I was the first day we started training. And now here he was discrediting all the progress I've made so far.

Fighting came surprisingly natural to me and I picked it up quickly, yet he still thought it was okay to undermine my ability simply because I was his mate and he could. Shouldn't this be the other way around? He should be proud of me for how strong I actually am! He knows my potential, but he's just being an huge asshole. I ignored the fact that practically everyone was snooping in on our little dispute.

"You don't get to tell me what I can and can't do! I am your mate and the Luna of this fucking pack as of a few weeks ago! If I want to fight alongside my warriors to protect our people, I fucking will!" I shrieked. My face felt flushed, and I knew my anger was visible. I could feel the pack's unease through the pack link. It was never a good thing when the Alpha and Luna fought.

He took a menacing step towards me, but I stood my ground. No way will I let him make me feel inferior. Not today, not ever.

"Yes, I do get a say in what you do! If I tell you you're not doing something, you're not fucking doing it! I am your Alpha and you will do as I fucking say!" He bellowed out with finality. I couldn't fucking believe he pulled the Alpha card. That was one low fucking blow. I felt my eyes sting with unshed tear, even though I wasn't even upset – just extremely angry. Too bad for him I always have to get the last word in everything.

"Well you know what? You may be the Alpha of this pack, but you are not the Alpha of this relationship! So you can just go-" I was about to let out a slew of curse words when my wolf forced herself forward and I shot my head towards the trees, searching them frantically. A wave of searing warmth rush through my body and without second thought I made a mad dash towards the trees. I ran as fast as I possibly could, only vaguely aware of the fact that my mate was just barely keeping up with my fleeting pace. I came to a stop at a clearing where a little girl, only about six or seven, was laying half alive on the grass in a pool of her own blood.

Releasing a feral growl, I dashed towards her body and began examining her wounds. She had deep claw marks marring her entire stomach and majority of her upper right leg. Packs usually never had an issue with rogues, or Wilds as most liked to call them, because they tended to be peaceful creatures living out the rest of their life in wolf form.

But, in this moment, I had no doubt that it was some filthy rogue who did this. No one else in his or her right mind would harm a sweet, innocent little girl. My hands started to tickle and itch as an aura of bright white light began to emanate from their skin. On instinct, I pressed and slid my radiating palms over the little girl's wounds and watched as her skin began to fuse back together perfectly, not even leaving a trace of a scar behind. Her once shallow breaths were beginning to deepen and her pale, white skin pinkening with color once again. I smiled from ear to ear when the little girls eyes opened once again and she stared back at me.

"Hi sweetheart. I'm Luna Aceso, can you tell me your name and what happened to you?" I asked in a quiet, soothing voice. I helped her sit up and she climbed into my lap with a little difficulty. I stroked her hair and whispered encouraging words in her ear before all the tension left her body and she finally spoke.

"I was c-chasing a butterfly for mama cause she always tells me how beautiful t-they are, but then some man with red eyes c-came out a-and when I asked him if he could h-help me get mama a butterfly he hurt me." She said, beginning to stutter as big, fat tears made an appearance.

"Why did he hurt m-me Luna Aceso?" She cried into my neck. My heart broke at how sad she sounded. My sorrow for the little girl, whose name I was informed through the pack link was apparently Mariposa, was instantly replaced with anger with the disgusting rogue. I finally glanced around the shocked crowd that eyes bore into me before calling for three of our warriors. I covered Mariposa's ears while I spoke.

"Luke, Jake, Steele! Gather a group and send out a search party. I don't want you back until that piece of fucking shit is dead, do you hear me?" I demanded, the natural Luna instincts inside of me coming out.

"Yes Luna." They all spoke simultaneously before dashing off into the surrounding forest.

Xavier's POV

"Well you know what? You may be the Alpha of this pack, but you are not the Alpha of this relationship! So you can just go-" I waited for the insults that never came. I watched as Aceso's hair began to glow once again and her once ocean blue eyes transformed into a bright silver. I mind linked for the pack doctor and Elder Esmeralda as she began frantically looking around the clearing. Just as they arrived, Aceso shot off into the trees. I tried my best to keep up with her, but it was difficult. I'd never met anyone who was even close to as fast as me, but here I was struggling to keep up with my mate's pace.

I watched in astonishment as we stopped at a clearing about a mile and a half away. There was a mauled little girl lying on the grass, bleeding out. My wolf's anger rushed through my body and I began to shake. Someone dare fucking harm one of my pack members!

A few minutes later everyone else joined us. We all stood around, watching in amazement as Aceso's hands began to match the glow of her hair and she literally healed the little girl that was practically dead on the forest floor. A woman, who I assumed was the little girl's mother went to run towards the two that were now cuddled in each other's embrace. I put my hand up to stop her. Obviously Aceso knew what she was doing right now and didn't need to be interrupted.

"Luke, Jake, Steele! Gather a group and send out a search party. I don't want you back until that piece of fucking shit is dead, do you hear me?" She spat out, making sure the little girl in her arms didn't hear the vulgar words she spoke. I couldn't help the pride I felt when I watched her taking on her Luna role like a complete natural. No one spoke a word after the warriors left to hunt down the rogue. It was finally Elder Esmeralda who broke the deafening silence.

"Just as I suspected. Alpha Xavier, Jarrod, Luna Aceso, we must talk in private. This is a highly confidential matter." She said, shooting us all a serious look before turning on her heels and making her way back to the pack house. We all nodded before Aceso handed the little girl back to her mother, who then continued to cry and thank he numerous times for saving her. I reached out to hold Aceso's hand as we walked, but she yanked her hand away from mine and walked ahead of me. I barely managed to suppress my wolf's rage due to her easy dismissal of me. I glared at the back of her head, fully knowing that she can feel my displeasure through our bond. She can be pissed off at me all she wants, but I will never allow her to fight.

Leighton's POV

I sat in my dad's office, staring off into space as my father continued to scream at me at the top of his lungs. He's been going on like this ever since I first walked in an hour ago.

"Are you even fucking listening to me, Leighton? You're a worthless piece of shit soon-to-be Alpha! I can't believe I have to hand down my position to someone so fucking un-qualified. You couldn't even follow one simple fucking order! You have ruined the entire plan! You were given one simple order to stay close to Aceso and not let her out of your sight, but what do you do? You let that fucking wannabe Alpha steal her right out from under your nose!" When he finished his tirade his chest was heaving up and down and his face was bright red with exertion. He pinched the bridge of his nose in annoyance as he stared me right in the eyes. Suddenly, a malicious smile spread across his face.

Shit.

"Because of your incompetence, your true mate is going to suffer. I have told you time and time again, if you don't follow instructions and do as your grandfather and I say, your mate would get your punishment instead. This is truly so sad, Leighton. She really is a such a sweet girl." He said, mocking me.

My heart crumbled at his words. I couldn't let them do this to my perfect Arabelle. My excuse of a father has been keeping my true mate captive since I found her three months ago while doing a border patrol. She was on a run and had accidentally stepped over our boundary line. I can't thank Goddess enough that it was I that had found her, and not someone else. Well, that's what I thought until I introduced her to my parents. I knew my dad and grandpa had this weird obsession with Aceso, but it wasn't until they forcefully separated me from Arabelle and locked her in the pack cells and they finally explained their plan to me that I realized just how sick the two of them were.

It was sick, really. The thought that they would actually fucking make me and Aceso mate forcefully just because of a hunch that they had. It was repulsive.

They didn't even know if she really was the next chosen healer or not! They were gambling with not only Aceso's life and our true mate's lives but also my life, his own son. My own father didn't have a single care in the world whether I died or not because of the forced mating. I became blinded by my hatred for my father and abruptly stood up before throwing the chair I was once sitting in across the room, causing it to shatter in the process.

"You can't do this dad! You can't keep me from my true mate just because you and grandfather are fucking power hungry mongrels! This is absolutely wrong and when the council finds out what you've done, and have been doing, you will be executed!" I screamed before storming out, knocking shoulders with my grandfather on the way.

I ran as fast as my legs would carry me through our pack land. I knew that a guard would soon alert my father that I was heading in the direction of Bloodlust territory, but I was hoping that I would be fast enough to get there before he came after me himself.

Chapter 15

A ceso's POV

I glanced between my father and Elder Esmeralda from my spot upon Xavier's lap. After the argument we had, this was the last place I wanted to be, but at the same time the elder's words had spooked me and the only one who was able to calm me was my mate.

There was a silent tenseness amongst us all as we waited for Alethia and her mate to join us. No one spoke, too afraid to break the eerie calm of the room.

"Jeez guys, who died?" Alethia questioned upon entering the room.

"There isn't time for jokes, Alethia. There is too much to discuss, too much at stake. Now, let me try and explain as best as I can. First, you all must know that what is said in this room, stays in this room. Not a single soul shall know about what is being said in here today." She rushed out, making eye contact with each and every one of us, letting us know how serious the situation actually was. I swallowed deeply, the fear I was feeling earlier returning with a vengeance.

"When Alethia and Aceso were first born, I – as well as all the other pack elders, had strong suspicion that they were moon blessed. There were far too many coincidences happening all at once; Jarrod and Lidia having troubles conceiving, but then suddenly Lidia was bearing twins. Not to mention the pups being fraternal, and both female. What came to be true was a thought on our radar, but it wasn't until the timing of their births and the timing of the previous Moon blessed wolves deaths that what we predicted came to be true." She trailed off cryptically.

"By Moon blessed do you mean..." My father said, eyes bugging from their sockets in disbelief. I glanced around, noticing that I wasn't the only one that was completely oblivious to the conclusion my father had come to.

"Yes, Jarrod." She said, a somewhat grim tone lacing her words.

"Can someone please explain what the hell is going on?" I begged, at my wits end. Xavier began rubbing circles into my flesh, trying to calm my rising tide of emotions.

"This is something that most parents are required to teach their children, but there was an obvious scheme in place to keep you in the dark Aceso. As for you, Alethia, I'm assuming it just slipped your parents' minds due to their grief." Elder Esmeralda said, giving my father a pointed look.

"There are two key components to our kind that keep us safe and from self-destruction. This being the two Moon blessed wolves: The healer and the Peacekeeper. There is only ever one living peacekeeper and healer wolf living at one time. They are the two wolves that the Moon herself watches over and keeps safe from any harm. The healer wolf travels to any pack that is having a major health tragedy. As you all know, this rarely happens due to our high immune systems, but it can happen. The healing instincts will come naturally and without warning. The sensation is said to be almost like an out-of-body experience, an individual is vaguely aware of their actions until after they have completed them."

"As far as the Peacekeeper wolf goes, it's pretty self explanatory. If there are any major imminent threats of war, they will be naturally guided there to solve the issue before it becomes a dangerous situation for those involved. As I stated before, the Elder's and I had strong suspicion that you girls were the next Moon blessed wolves, which is why we chose the name we did for Alethia. You are named after the Goddess of truth. We also know now the reason for Aceso's kidnapping. We believe the Nightshade pack elders caught wind of the same information we did and took whichever child they could get ahold of. Their reasoning for it is still unclear as of right now, but we've come to this conclusion due to them naming Aceso after the Goddess of curing or healing."

Once she had finished, she sat back in her seat, looking just as tense but almost relieved in a way to have finally shared such a large piece of information.

"How could the Moon let Aceso be kidnapped? If she is supposedly watching over and personally protecting her blessed children, why would she let something like that happen?" Xavier asked heatedly, obviously angry with what I had been through.

"She is here now. We cannot question why the Moon does the things she does, we just have to learn to embrace them and thank her for the things she is kind enough to bless us with." Elder Esmeralda said. Xavier cocked one of his eyebrows up in a defiant manner, to which I slapped his arm for. He narrowed his eyes at me before I gave him a reprimanding look and mouthed to word "stop".

"So, you're saying Aceso and I are in charge of keeping the entirety of werewolf kind from being totally fucked?" Alethia questioned bluntly. Elder Esmeralda bristled slightly at her choice of words causing me to stifle my laughed against Xavier's neck.

"I guess you could put it that way." She said reluctantly.

"What a horrible choice on her behalf. My mother still does my laundry." Alethia joked. I couldn't contain my laughter from bubbling from my chest, but the elder harshly slapping her hand against the desk sobered me up instantly.

"This is serious, girls!" She scolded angrily.

"I understand that, and I'm sorry Elder. You have to understand that we're just trying to make light of a very heavy situation. Having something like this thrust upon us at random is quite a lot to take in all at once." I said somberly, pleading her with my eyes to understand.

She released a heavy sigh. "I get that, which is why I've already called for the mostly highly respected members that belong to the same pack as the previous wolves to come and help you out and possibly give you a few pointers. They understand the severity of keeping this situation very quiet. They shall be here within the next few days.

"Are we going to report the kidnapping to the council?" My mother asks softly.

"No." My dad says immediately. "I'm going to take out that entire fucking pack personally. The ground will be soaked in their blood and I will enjoy every goddamn second of it. They will pay for what they put us through." He finalized, eyes darkening with a feral gleam that sent a shiver of fear down my spine. Xavier realized my unease and released a low growl, warning my father to stop before he made him.

"So does this mean I'm safe? Why do we have to keep all of this a secret if we're both protected by the Moon?" I questioned, somewhat at a loss.

"We cannot be sure what the Nightshades are planning. They've gone against the Moon once; I wouldn't put it past them to do it again. It's best just to lay low. It is better to be safe than sorry." Esmeralda explained. I nodded in understanding.

Suddenly, the door burst open as five of our main border patrol guards stormed in.

"I'm sorry to interrupt, Alpha and Luna, but there's been a border breach in the south...he's demanding to speak to the Luna." The guard said uneasily. Xavier released a deep, threatening growl before shielding my entire body with his own massive form.

"Did they give a name? What did they look like?" I asked, trying to be the rational one between the two of us.

"He's a few inches taller than I and had brown hair. Said you would know it was urgent. His name was Lucas or something like that." The guard said, scrunching his forehead as he searched his mind for his name.

"Leighton?" I questioned, my heart pounding furiously.

"Yeah! That was it. He's already been thrown in the cells for now. You can decide what you want done with him later, Alpha." He said, ignoring me completely.

"Execute him immediately." Xavier demanded.

"NO!" I screamed, trying to stand, but before forced to stay sitting due to Xavier's heavy arms holding me down. He growled in my ear at my refusal.

"You can't execute him! He's my best friend! He has to be here for a reason! I need to see him!" I said.

"You aren't seeing that fucker. Not now, not ever. We are going back to our room and they are going to execute him." Xavier said with finality. Everyone in the room squirmed, uncomfortable with witnessing their leaders fighting.

"If you execute him I will never speak to you ever again! I will never look at you ever again!" I seethed, digging my nails into the skin of his forearm while shooting daggers at him with my eyes.

"Leave him be for the night and we will discuss what happens to him later. You are dismissed. Lets go." Xavier said, hauling me up off the couch and dragging me out of the office towards our bedroom by my bicep.

Once inside, Xavier slammed the door, nearly breaking it off its hinges, before turning to glare at me.

"Don't give me that look, you fucking prick! I can't believe you would just try and kill my best friend without giving a single thought to how that would fucking make me feel!" I yelled, balling my hands into fists and squeezing.

"I don't give a fuck about that son of a bitch! If he's a nightshade, he dies. End of story." He hissed back. Tears pricked my eyes. Who is this man before me?

"How can you say that? I get killing the high-ranking wolves and making them pay for what they did, but you can't just go killing a bunch of innocent people! That makes you no better than Alpha Jack!" I accused. Xavier released a menacing laugh at my words.

"I don't give a fuck. All I care about is making sure you're safe. I'll kill anyone and anything that threatens that." He said. I released the tears that I had been holding back, unable to control my emotions. His face softened instantly.

"Baby-" he started to say, but I spun on my heels and made a mad dash for the bathroom before locking myself in. He banged on the door, begging me to let him in. I ignored him, turning the shower on and getting in to hopefully drown out his pleading.

Eventually, he gave up. I exited the bathroom, too mentally exhausted to do anything but sleep. I assumed Xavier went back to training and thanked my lucky stars. I didn't want anything to do with him at the moment.

Slipping into one of his large t-shirts, I climbed into our bed and relaxed as Xavier's strong scent wrapped around my body, overwhelming my senses.

Chapter 16

A ceso's POV

I lay in Xavier and I's bed, trying my best to force my mind to shut off so that I could fall asleep. The fact that it's only late afternoon, I haven't had dinner (something my growling stomach just informed me of), and the fact that Xavier is plaguing my thoughts has made my attempts practically impossible. He's such a stupid, stupid man. Thinks he can just growl at me and flash his canines to get his way. I think fucking not.

With a frustrated groan, I heave myself up and cross my arms over my chest in frustration as my feet dangle over the side of the bed. I wanted to scream I was so pissed off, but I could also cry, but I also really fucking wanted some pancakes. With chocolate chips. Maybe even some peanut butter on top. Or all three combined... yes, that sounds divine right about now.

My mouth watered as I made my way down to the kitchen. I wanted to laugh that with everything going on in my life right now, my number one priority had become making myself a giant heaping plate of pancakes, devouring them, and then sleeping for the next 48 hours. I was just so tired. Swinging the refrigerator door open I began grabbing all the ingredients that I needed to make my food fantasy a reality. I was in the middle of mixing the batter when my phone began going off, the annoying alarm ringtone blaring throughout the kitchen. I quickly wiped my hands off on a towel and picked it up, nearly shitting myself when I read the message sprawled across my screen.

BUY TAMPONS!

Fuck! I can't believe I nearly forgot! Thank God I set myself a reminder, otherwise I would've totally forgot that my period was coming in about a week and I had yet to stock up on all my lady products since arriving at my true birth pack. I was about to send Alethia a quick text asking if she had some extra stuff I could steal just in case I wasn't able to make it to the store amongst all the shit that was going on as of right now, but then Xavier sauntered into the kitchen. I bristled towards him before turning my back to him and plopping a dollop of batter onto the pan that'd been heating up.

"Aceso." He barked out, trying to get my attention. He was clearly annoyed with my ignorance of his presence. He released a deep sigh before rounding the kitchen island and leaning his hip against the counter right next to where I was cooking.

"Baby, you have to understand." He tried once again, but I was having none of it. I didn't have to understand jack shit. He wanted to mercilessly execute one of my best friends without a single regard to how that would make me feel. It's not that I don't understand where he's coming from in his need to protect me, but there's absolutely no reason for him to kill Leighton. Not when he risked his ass to come here and see me for what I knew was a very serious reason. What he didn't know was that I have full intentions of waiting until he was dead asleep tonight to sneak out and go visit him in his holding cell. I knew the idea itself was fucking stupid, which is why I intended to take a few guards with me. There were a couple that I knew were more empathetic than most of the lot, so I intended to use that knowledge to my advantage.

"You can go back to training." I replied in a monotone voice. He growled out his frustration before stomping back out through the way he came. I continued to happily cook myself my hot cakes while humming a light tune when the repulsive scent of seafood engulfed me. I gagged before pulling the pan I was cooking on off the range top and slapped a hand over my mouth. I tried to get my convulsing stomach under control as a large group of people entered the kitchen with various bags of shrimp and oysters in their hands. I could feel the bile quickly creeping up my throat as I made a mad dash for the bathroom. I was on my knees in seconds, yacking up the large breakfast I'd had earlier that morning.

Definitely not as appealing coming up as it went down.

I continued to retch until there wasn't anything left in my poor, battered stomach. Still, even then, the lingering smell of seafood was enough to have my head hovering over the toilet bowl. Someone incessantly knocked at the bathroom door.

"Luna? Luna, are you okay? I'm going to get the Alpha, stay put!" I yelled out a quick no and grimaced at the absolutely vile aftertaste that consumed my mouth. Unfortunately, I didn't have enough energy to haul myself up off the floor to rinse my mouth out with mouthwash. It was as if every ounce of energy that I had in my body rushed out all at once, leaving me to slump my body against the hunk of porcelain in front of me and close my heavy eyelids.

I couldn't even bring myself to open my eyes when I heard the bathroom door opening and closing quietly. My mother's comforting scent flooded the room – effectively removing the disgusting fishy smell – before she crouched down next to me.

"Sweetheart? Can you hear me?" She cooed out while placing a dainty hand atop my head and stroking my hair lovingly. I responded with an incoherent groan before heaving out a sigh. I was just so fucking tired. But I also really wanted those pancakes. Before I knew it, tears were dribbling down my face uncontrollably.

"I j-just want my p-pancakes." I spoke through a sob. She laughed lightly in response before wrapping her arm around my waist and pulling my arm around her shoulder and helping me up. She guided me into the kitchen once again – which I knew for a fact had been dowsed in Lysol due to the hospital-like smell – before requesting help from one of the many men to carry me upstairs.

"Wait! My pancakes!" I yelled as my eyebrows furrowed in distress, still not opening my eyes.

"I know, honey, I'll make a plate and bring them up so you can eat them in bed." I relaxed instantly and let the random male scoop me up into his arms as he carried me upstairs.

"This is as far as I can go, Luna. The Alpha will have my head if I enter your personal quarters." His tone was nervous, but still professional.

"Mhmmm, thank you." I mumbled, blindly reaching up to pat his cheek in thanks. I felt my way along the wall to my bedroom door before throwing it open and wandering about, hoping my body will make contact with our huge bed sometime soon.

My wish was granted as I smacked my right shin into the base of our bed, screaming a slew of profanities directly after. After nursing what I knew was going to be a gigantic bruise, I launched myself on the bed and snuggled in, smiling as my wolf settled down in my head due to our mate's scent.

"Sweetheart, you're going to have to sit up if you want to eat these otherwise you'll get syrup all over." I finally cracked my eyes open at her words and meandered up in bed, my stomach releasing an embarrassingly loud growl as I set my sights on the huge pile of pancakes before me. Not that I cared - at all.

I completely ignored what was going on around me as I devoured almost all of the food in ten minutes flat. I felt so much more awake after getting a decent amount of food in my body. My mom stayed around to chat for about twenty minutes before she needed to leave and help Alethia pack her things to move in with Rory.

I sat in silence for about five minutes before my thoughts started up. I usually never get sick, so today was a little weird for me. Normally, the week before my period I just really emotional. I wonder if Xavier would be the type of guy to say fuck it and have sex while I was on my period with a condom, or completely avoid me down there. I giggled at the thought of him having to go without because he'd royally pissed me off. Even if he wanted to have sex he'd have to go to the store and get condoms. Talk about inconvenient.

Wait.

Wait.

OH FUCK! I scrambled up off the bed and tore through not only my suitcase, but also Xavier's. To my absolute utter horror, I found a box of condoms in his suitcase. An unopened box of condoms.

Unopened.

Shit, shit, shit, shit, shit.

I ran into the bathroom and dropped to my knees as I searched under the cabinet frantically. I knew my mom said they always kept an abundance of pregnancy tests in the pack house because there was always at least one girl getting knocked up. Males just couldn't keep it in their pants - like ever.

Coming up short, I cursed to myself as I left our room and raided the next bathroom I came upon. Thank god there was a single test left in the pack of five I found in the medicine cabinet. It was even one of those fancy and expensive ones too, where it says "pregnant" or "not pregnant" instead of leaving you to try and interpret what a single pink fucking line means.

Hooking my fingers into my my yoga pants, I shoved them down my legs along with my underwear before popping the lid off the test and placing my hand between my legs. Fuck, this is so uncomfortable. How do people do this? I scrunched my nose up as I got a little bit of pee on my hand. I capped the lit on the glorified pee stick and finished doing my business and washing my hands. I set a timer on my phone for the recommended five minutes and tried my best to ignore the jitters in my stomach as I aimlessly played around on my phone.

I jumped the slightest bit and dropped my phone in shock when the timer went off. I felt like my stomach was in my throat as I tried to calm my shaking hands. Picking up the test, I looked to the sky and prayed. For what, I have absolutely no idea. Pregnant? Not pregnant? Having Xavier's baby would be a dream come true. It really would, but right now is so not the right time for it. We had yet to get everything with the Nightshade pack sorted, and bringing a baby into the whole mess would only further complicate things.

But now that I was thinking about it, I wanted it. Fuck I wanted it so bad. A baby. A baby with the man I love - even if he is huge dickhead sometimes. No matter what happened, I would love my children with everything I had. I would do everything in my power to keep my child out of harms way. With that thought in my I took a deep breath and glanced at the piece of plastic in my hands.

Pregnant.

My mind raced. I felt light headed. Shit. I still felt how I felt about a whopping five seconds ago, but this made this 1000x more real. I was fucking pregnant. I had Xavier's child growing inside me. Tears pricked my eyes. I was so happy, but so damn scared. That fucking prick probably knew! He unloaded his man juice inside me while I was in heat and didn't even say anything! God damn him! With everything going on I didn't even consider the possibility of me being pregnant. That's probably why he tensed up so quickly when we started talking about kids all those weeks ago. That little fucker.

I was seething. If I was a cartoon, there would be steam rising from my ears right now. First things first, I needed to go to the pack doctor and make sure this was the real deal, figure out how far along I was and get my vitamins and all that good stuff. Then, then I can tear Xavier a new one for not saying anything. Boy, did he have some shit coming.

Wandering into the pack clinic, which was conveniently in the basement of the left wing of the pack house, I tried my best to return the doctor's friendly smile.

"Hi, Luna! What brings you here this evening?" She said, her tone light and inviting.

"This." I said, whipping out the pregnancy test. I had decided it was best to just address the situation head on instead of beating around the bush. Her eyes widened for a fraction of a second before a huge smile that reached her eyes lit up her face. She squealed in delight before engulfing me in a huge hug.

"I'm so happy for you and the Alpha! Oh! The pack will be ecstatic! Come, let's get an ultrasound and figure out how far along you are." She bounced about, and extra pep in her step as she set up all her big, fancy equipment. By the way she's acting, you would think she was the one who just found out she was knocked up.

I couldn't deny that it all felt a little wrong having my first ultrasound without Xavier by my side. The little niggling of guilt tore at my conscious as I lifted my stomach for her before letting out a little squeak as the ice-cold gel hit my stomach. I brushed the feeling away, deciding it was better to be 100% sure that this was the real deal before getting Xavier's hopes up.

Suddenly, a rapid whooshing noise ricocheted around the room bringing tears to my eyes.

"That's your baby's heartbeat! Very strong!" She gushed while examining the screen. I stared at the black and white blob of what to someone else would've been nothing, but to me it was absolutely everything. This was my first time seeing my precious little baby, Xavier and I's proof of our love. Tears cascaded down my cheeks as I sat in the chair blubbering like a fool.

"Okay, I'm going to print you a picture and then we'll get down to the nitty gritty stuff." She spoke while wiping the gel from my stomach. I nodded my head and watched her go, my heart beating a mile a minute. The sound of my little one's beating heart will be engraved into my heart until my last breath. I reached my hands down and caressed my miniscule little bump that I so stupidly brushed off as bloating. The edges of my lips tugged up into a smile as the thought of Xavier chasing our toddler around the kitchen while I cook breakfast, or watching him teach them to play sports.

My train of thought was cut off as the doctor, who's name I gathered was Emily from the degrees proudly hung upon the wall, reentered the room with a couple bottle of pills and a envelope.

"This is your ultrasound picture," she said raising her hand that held the envelope, "and these are some various pills you'll need. Prenatal vitamins, pills for severe morning sickness – which tends to happen in a lot of Alpha pregnancies – and some extra nutrition pills. You'll need all the energy you can possibly get while pregnant. That baby will suck every last ounce of energy you have as you get farther into your pregnancy. Now, we'll need to discuss the logistics of how this is going to work, because it's a little different from human pregnancies and they don't teach you this stuff in school." She said while settling down in her rolling chair.

"Now, while werewolf pregnancies last just as long as human pregnancies, that's really the only thing we have in common with humans. One month of a human pregnancy, growth wise, is equivalent to one and a half months of werewolf pregnancy. This means you'll be at full term size wise at around six months. The remaining three months of your pregnancy is the time when your baby's inner wolf is developing." She laughed at my expression, which I knew was completely blank face. Why the hell weren't they teaching us this shit in school? This is something I would've liked to have known!

"As far as how far along you are in your pregnancy, based upon your ultrasound results today I'd estimate you at about two and a half weeks along. Your due date will be sometime in October, though we can't be too sure because werewolf due dates are very touch and go. I've put you down in my schedule for another check up appointment two weeks from today. If something comes up before there, feel free to come visit me or send someone to get me. Otherwise I look forward to seeing you soon!"

I couldn't even reply to her, just smiled and nodded. Anything I had to say got caught in my throat. It wasn't until I got about 10 steps out of the office that my anger hit me like a fucking brick wall. Hot and searing, it scorched my insides until I felt like I would self-combust. My light, airy walk turned into purposeful stomping strides as I made my way upstairs. I heard loud bouts of laughter and deep voices yelling at one another coming from the entertainment room, which meant training was over. Stepping in, I must have looked like one real fucking pissed off bitch because every single warrior, even Beta Aaron, adverted their gaze to the floor and bore their neck to me in submission.

"Aaron, where the fuck is Xavier?" I spat out. He cringed as if I had slapped him across the face.

"Did you need something, baby?" Xavier's voice spoke from the doorway. I spun on my heels, shooting daggers at him with my eyes. He furrowed his brow as he inspected the items in my hands.

"Don't you fucking 'baby' me you dickhead! You knew I was pregnant this whole time didn't you! I can't believe you kept this from me! I'm going for a walk, get your shit before I'm back because you aren't sleeping with me tonight." I screamed, finally taking a much needed deep breath before shoving past him on my way out, completely ignoring Xavier's yells for me to stop.

Chapter 17

Aceso's POV

I wandered around our pack lands, fully aware of the six – yes six – pack warriors following closely behind. The entire 30 minutes I was out, my tears never stopped. If this was what pregnancy was like - crying uncontrollably all the time and fucking always feeling hungry - then I was in for a long ass nine months. Every time I stopped crying, I would think about one of four things: Xavier pissing me off by keeping so many important details from me, Xavier threatening to kill my best friend, Leighton being held up in some dank cell even though he poses no threat to me, and my perfect little baby.

I began to grow tired, my eyelids starting to droop for the second time today. My stomach began to feel empty and in need of something - what exactly I wasn't quite sure of just yet - but on top of all that, what I needed the most was someone to talk to.

Alethia, where are you? I mind linked, hoping she wasn't still busy packing her things.

In the kitchen making myself something to eat, what's wrong? Oh thank God I thought to myself.

Be there in a minute. Make enough for two...wait make that three. I said before cutting off the connection. Despite my lack of energy, I speed walked to the kitchen, eager to get some food into my grumbling stomach. The smell of pasta hit my nose as soon as I stepped through the doorway and I moaned my appreciation.

"Wow, you got here fast." She said, amusement lacing her tone. She looked behind me before a slight frown pulled at her lips. "Wait, where's Xavier? I thought you said make enough for three?"

"I did." I said, swallowing the large lump in my throat as I waited for her to understand. It took her longer than I expected, so I figured she could use an additional hint. I lifted my hand and placed it over my tiny little bump and rubbing it in soothing circles. Her eyes grew wide as saucers and she choked on her own spit.

"Y-you're pregnant?!" She gasped out, jaw slackened in shock. I nodded my head slowly, unsure of how to interpret her reaction. It wasn't good, but it wasn't exactly bad either. Just, well, shocked. Then, she did something that surprised the hell out of me. She threw her head back and let out a loud, hysterical laugh.

"What's so funny?" I asked, suddenly feeling defensive for no reason.

"Because this means mom and dads bet is a tie." She spoke through small giggles. I blinked at her a few times, completely unaware as to what the hell she was talking about.

"Mom and dad made a bet that you would get pregnant before I would. Jokes on them, I just found out three days ago. I wasn't sure the best way to tell the family." Her face was the perfect picture of amusement as she watched my emotion rapidly change from confusion to shock.

"Holy shit! You've got a bun cooking too?" She just laughed and nodded her head.

"Rory can't keep his hands to himself. To be fair, I can't either. Every time we go to lie down for bed he gives me a kiss goodnight, and every night it always turns into something more, so much more. I swear, you think I would learn by now to just peck his cheek and call it good." She said, rolling her eyes at herself. I laughed loudly, knowing exactly what she meant.

"Sounds just like Xavier. Except that isn't what got me in this situation in the first place." I spat, my anger resurfacing for the nth time tonight.

"What do you mean?" She asked eying me warily. I sniffled as my eyes began to fill with tears. Jesus Christ, not this again.

"H-he lied to me. He d-didn't tell me t-that we didn't use a c-condom during my heat. H-he knew and never t-told me!" I blubbered.

"Oh, honey." Alethia spoke out on a sigh, wrapping her arms around me and rubbing comforting circles into the small of my back. She pulled away, only to return moments later with a plate overflowing with what looked like lasagna amongst other things. I quickly shoved a large bite into my mouth and moaned, ignoring the fact that I probably had third degree burns on my tongue now.

"Holy shit, this is so good, Lee." I praised. She mumbled a quiet 'mhmm' through her own mouthful. That was the end of the conversation as we both became preoccupied with our plates of food. It wasn't until our mother wandered into the kitchen that we finally spoke again.

"Aceso, sweetie, what happened? What's wrong?" I furrowed my brow until I realized my makeup was probably streaked all down my face, and my eyes were probably red and puffy too. Instead of giving her an answer, I took the ultra sound picture out of the envelope as well as pulling the pregnancy test from my pocket. She grabbed them from my hands and frantically moved her eyes from me to them. She choked on a sob as she threw her arms around me.

"I'm going to be a grandma!" She squealed in delight.

"Make that times two..." Alethia added quietly before rounding the counter and coming to stand next to us.

"You two are going to give me a heart attack." She wept, voice cracking at the end of her sentence.

"Will you sleep with me tonight, mom? I don't wanna sleep alone." I whimpered like an infant. She jerked her head back, a look of utter confusion on her face.

"What are you on about? Xavier is here, is he not?" She said, eyes scanning my face.

"Yes, but we got into a fight. He's known I was pregnant this entire time and never uttered a single word to me about it. I didn't know he didn't use protection...that night. We made a promise to each other that we'd never keep anything from one another, no matter how big or small. He broke that promise already and I don't want to see him for the rest of the night." I huffed acting half my age.

"Sweetie, don't you think you're blowing this a little out of proportion?" She questioned carefully as to not anger me.

"Of course I know I'm making this bigger than it needs to be, but dammit I'm mad and I just want to wallow in my misery without him tonight!" I yelled. My mother threw her head back and laughed before nodding her head.

"I guess that's alright. Your father will be very upset, but I never got to cuddle with my other baby and I want to tonight. Both of you. I can kick your father out and tell him he has to sleep in the guest room tonight." She finalized. I squealed in excitement. All I'd ever wanted in my life was my mate, and my mom. Now I would finally get a chance to have both of those things.

I said my parting words before dashing off to my bedroom to take a quick shower and change into some pajamas. Blatantly ignoring Xavier's huge imposing frame sitting at the edge of our bed, I walked right past him and quickly stripped before stepping under the hot spray. I was in the middle of massaging the shampoo into my scalp when I felt the familiar hardness of Xavier's chest press into me from behind. I let out a low growl as he pushed my hands away, but it soon turned into a moan as his strong fingers began massaging my scalp, applying the perfect amount of pressure. My body turned into jelly as I leaned all my weight against him, fully enjoying the pleasure he was keen on giving me.

He carefully turned me so my head was under the water before giving my forehead a sound kiss. Once all the suds were gone from my hair, he turned me once more and repeated the process all over again, but with conditioner. I laid my head against his chest, the rhythmic beating of his heart lulling me into a half asleep, half awake state. His hands were firm against my skin as he lathered and rubbed my body all over. There wasn't anything sexual about the act. It was simply him taking care of his mate; making sure I was happy and comfortable. When he was done rinsing me completely off, he cradled me in his arms while running his nose up and down my neck.

"I'm sorry." He whispered against my skin, so quiet I could just barely hear it. "I'm so sorry. I didn't want to freak you out with everything else that was already going on. I wasn't even sure if my suspicion was right or not." He said, swallowing audibly when I didn't reply right away. I released a deep sigh before angling my head back so I could meet his eyes before cupping his face between my hands.

"I know." I breathed out against his lips. He made the first move of leaning down and capturing my lips with his own. I responded immediately, opening my lips the slightest to allow his tongue access to explore. He tasted so damn good all the time. It was one that I knew I was addicted to and would never kick the habit of wanting.

"Let's go to bed." He murmured, his chest rising and falling rapidly. I shook my head back and forth, almost laughing at how quickly his body tensed up.

"I promised my mom and my sister I would have a sleep-over with them. Some mom/sister/daughter bonding time of sorts." The tension left his body, but I could tell he was still uneasy.

"Fine, but tomorrow you're mine. I want you to myself all day so we can talk about everything."

"On one condition." I said, putting my finger to his lips as soon as he opened them to protest.

"I want you to take me to see Leighton tomorrow at the pack cells. He poses no threat to my wellbeing. He's been my best friend since before I can even remember and the fact that he even dared step onto Bloodlust territory lets me know that he's in some sort of trouble and needs my help. If you love me, you'll help me help him." I said, giving him my hardest set of eyes – letting him know there was no room for negotiation.

He released a loud growl, "Fine, but I'm not happy about this. At all. And we go in with warriors surrounding you, or we don't go in at all." I wrapped my arms around his neck and jumped up, squeezing my legs around his waist while whispering my words of thanks in his ear.

Bad idea.

He spun and pinned my back up against the shower wall, positioning his already rock hard dick against my entrance.

"Wait! No! I don't want to face my mother and sister smelling all sexed up!" I said, slapping his shoulder.

"Please? You can spray yourself with perfume. They'll never know." He said, running the head of his cock up and down my dripping slit. I released a feral moan before moving my hips just enough to push the head of his monstrous length just inside of me. Fuck, he felt so good.

Grabbing my ass in his hands, he thrust all the way into me. He was so deep, he was brushing up against my cervix and holy shit did it feel good. I released a strangled cry of pleasure as he pulled out, only to ram back into me all over again. His punishing pace brought me to a quick release as I curled my toes and clawed at his back. His name was the only thing on my lips as he continued to pump in and out of me jerkily, desperately seeking his own release. When it finally came, the delicious sensation of his hot seed soaking my inner walls milked a second orgasm from my own body.

Feeling completely spent, he pulled out with a groan before gently setting me back down on the shower floor. My legs were completely useless and I clung to Xavier for dear life.

Turning the shower off, he carried me out before setting me down on the counter and proceeding to dry me off. One dry, he laid me on our bed before grabbing a pair of his boxers and one of his t-shirts and slipping it over my head. He squatted down to pull the boxers up my legs before he noticed a trail of his essence slowly dripping down my leg. Wiping it up with a single finger, he popped it in my mouth. His eyes heated up as I swirled my tongue around the digit. He released a wanton growl before tugging the boxers up my legs.

"There. They won't have a clue why you reek of me. Now go before I decide not to let you leave our bed." He rumbled out, voice deeper than usual and twice as husky.

Chapter 18

A I shot up in bed, quickly scrambling off and making a beeline for the bathroom. Dropping onto my knees, I just barely made it to the toilet bowl before spewing my guts everywhere. That's the last time I'll ever eat lasagna. I thought bitterly as I gagged just from the disgusting smell alone. I thought back to the pills Emily had prescribed me and kept cursing myself over and over for not taking one. My baby would never develop properly unless my body got enough nutrients and that wasn't going to happening if I was throwing up everything I ate at all times of the day.

"You're going to have to take the pills, honey. I was the exact same way with you and Lee. It was four straight months of eating and then throwing it right back up a couple hours later." I shuddered at the horrible thought of having to endure this shit for four straight months. I would never have survived that. I'm only about three days in and I'm already waving my white flag.

"What the hell is going on? Are you sick, angel?" My dad's deep voice floated into the bathroom from the doorway. My mom went to open her big mouth and blab about my pregnancy, but she stopped the second I lightly punched her leg. Her eyes flew to me and she gave me a pointed look that said, 'If you ever pull that shit again I'll make you regret being born'. I mouthed the word 'don't' and she released a heavy sigh before nodding in agreeance. "Well?" My dad prodded again, tapping his foot impatiently on the tile floor.

"What's going on? Oh, Cece, did you not take those pills yet?"

"Jesus, lets just make me throwing up a family function why don't we?" I gritted out between clenched teeth.

"You're my little girl, I have every right to be worried when I come in to see you throwing up. Especially when you were all fine when I left last night." I smiled at his words. Left is an understatement. We had to force him out of the room.

"What? This is my bedroom, you can't kick me out!" He yelled playfully.

"Well that's exactly what we're doing Jarrod. I want mother/daughter bonding and that can't happen with you here. Plus none of the spare rooms have beds big enough to comfortably fit three people." My mom explained while tossing him his pillow.

"I tell you what, an ungrateful bunch is what you all are." He teased before entering the ensuite closet/bathroom to change into his pajamas and brush his teeth. While he was getting ready to leave, we were getting comfortable in bed. Alethia and I both snuggled into our mom before giggling and wrapping our arms around each other. A slight sniffle and the clearing of a throat caught our attention and we all looked up. Dad stood near the foot of the bed with tears in his eyes, watching us.

"Dad, don't cry! There's only room for three girls in the room right now." Alethia had teased him.

"You shut that smart little mouth, young lady. Men can be sensitive, too." He said pointedly as he grabbed his things and wandered over to press a kiss to all three of our heads before finally leaving.

Not that you could really classify "leaving" as walking out the door, changing into wolf form, and then laying in front of the door like that all night. Not that any of us were going to comment on it.

"Sweetie, you need to tell him. He's your father." My mom whispered quietly enough that only the two of us heard it.

"I know. I had full intentions on telling him, just not while my head is in the toilet." I explained, still feeling incredibly nauseous. She helped me up before handing me a spare toothbrush and some toothpaste. Once finished I joined everyone in the bedroom, glancing at Alethia and knowing exactly how we both wanted to break this to our father.

"So you both lost the bet." I said glancing between my mom and dad.

"What are you on about, angel?" My dad asked, clearly confused.

"You and mom both lost the bet. Me and Alethia are both pregnant." I said, in a no bullshit mood. Alethia and I both watched as four separate emotions flittered across his face, one after another.

First shock, then happiness, excitement, and finally anger.

"Oh Jarrod come off of it! You've been talking about wanting to be a grandpa for years. How did you think that was going to happen? Immaculate conception?" My mom huffed while rolling her eyes.

"Just because I wanted grandkids doesn't mean I have to be happy about the way they were conceived, pumpkin." My dad said to my mom, totally miffed. She waved her hand in the air as if dismissing his comment altogether and bounced to her feet.

"This is going to be so exciting! We can go baby shopping and get the rooms all set up so that you both aren't too stressed out when the time comes." My mom gushed, her happiness almost palpable.

"Whoa, pumpkin, calm down. Give the girls some room to breathe, yeah?" The light in her eyes dimmed just the slightest bit as she nodded.

"Actually, that sounds perfect. I don't want to have to rush around to get everything done last minute. That kind of stress won't be good for the baby." I said to which Alethia quickly agreed. "Unfortunately, I can't go today. Xavier promised he'd take me to see Leighton in the pack cells to figure out why he came running here in the first place." Before I could even finish my sentence, a menacing growl ripped through the room. I released a defeated sigh, knowing that that reaction was a given from my father.

"There's no way in fucking hell you are going into that building! Especially not now that you're pregnant. Christ, Aceso, are you trying to dig your old man an early grave?"

He spoke as he gnashed he teeth together while rubbing at his temples. My chest became heavy with emotion.

"N-no, I just wanted to see my best friend and make sure he's okay." I stuttered out through the large lump that'd formed in my throat. I didn't wait for him to reply, because I knew for a fact it would just be him giving me another reason as to why I shouldn't and wouldn't be going to see Leighton.

Entering Xavier's office, I suddenly became aware of how ridiculous I looked dressed in nothing but Xavier's shirt (which was so long on me that you couldn't tell I was wearing pants) and his boxers as the other occupants of the room looked me up and down. Xavier's loud, possessive growl tore through the room, causing every male's eyes to either drop or advert to anything in the room that wasn't me.

"What is it, baby girl?" He said, his voice deep and raspy like it always was. I almost forgot what I needed because of all the dirty thoughts that started running through my head.

I cleared my throat, trying to push my embarrassment aside before speaking. "I want to go see Leighton now."

Chapter 19

Xavier's eyes turned cold the instant my words registered with him.

"Please?" I beg, mustering up the best puppy dog eyes I could manage. His cold exterior melted instantly. Bingo.

"Sweetheart, can it wait until a little later? I'd like to tie up some loose ends I've been meaning to take care of within the pack." He tried reasoning, but I knew he just really didn't want me in those cells. Well, that's just really too damn bad.

"But I know Leighton has to be in huge trouble otherwise he would've never come here. I know I wouldn't. You're kind of a cock sucker sometimes." I huffed, crossing my arms over my chest. I heard simultaneous snorts of laughter, a single pissed off growl, and the clearing of throats.

"Fine, we'll go to the God damned cells." He growled out, completely frustrated with me. I gigged to myself, knowing how thankful I am to have someone who loves me as much as he does while also putting up with my abundance of shit.

I lean up, pecking his cheek after he walked around desk to stand next to me. "I love you." I say with conviction. The tension in his body fades and he wraps his arm around my waist.

"I know, baby. Let's go see your friend." He said, before kissing me hard on the lips.

I now know why no one wanted me in these cells. I also now understand the saying, "out of sight, out of mind" and, "ignorance is bliss". Dear God, I wish I could be ignorant about all the things I've seen in the short few minutes we've been navigating these cells. I was practically plastered to Xavier's side, completely overwhelmed and scared. I knew it was killing him to want to say 'I told you so', but he's refrained from doing so the whole time, and for that I'm thankful.

"It's coming up on the right." Xavier muttered against my ear, giving my hip a reassuring squeeze. I swallowed the giant lump in my throat. We came up on one of the nice looking cells. I knew it wasn't intentional, but I'm at least glad this corner didn't smell overwhelmingly like mold.

It was dark enough that I could only see about two feet into the cell. I tried to step closer to get a better look inside the cell, but Xavier's hand instantly restricted the movement. I looked up at him questioningly, but knew not to push it too much when he game me such hard eyes. Xavier cleared his throat, which caused some rustling inside the cell.

"Come to interrogate me again?" Came a gruff, but familiar voice. I gasped as Leighton's imposing, well what I used to think was imposing before I met Xavier, frame came into view. He looked completely exhausted and spent.

"Leighton?" I cried softly, making a run for the cell. His head snapped up, eyes meeting mine as a look of surprise flashed across his face. I was two seconds away from meeting him at the bars and brushing my hands across his scruffed up face when a loud roar echoed through the building, causing all the walls to shake.

"Xavier, stop it!" I hissed, totally pissed off.

"Don't worry about it, Cece. If I were in the same boat as him, I'd do the exact same thing. Especially if my mate just so happened to be pregnant." He said, giving me a smug look.

I blushed a deep red before responding. "Shut up." I muttered. Leighton laughed at my discomfort before he was cut off by Xavier's growl.

"State what you fucking came here for." He demanded, obviously not wanting me around Leighton for another second.

"Xavier, quit being so rude. You're talking to the future Alpha of Nightshade pack. You could at least show a little respect." I scolded harshly.

A lighthearted chuckle coming from Leighton's cell caught me off guard. I swiveled my eyes to him in confusion.

"Aceso, you're the only person I know that would demand their mate, who just so happens to be an Alpha, to be polite to the future Alpha of his enemy pack." He shook his head as an amused smile graced his face.

"Whatever. You know our packs are only enemies because of your stupid father and grandfather. We have the chance to take them down and solve all these issues." I stated matter-of-factly.

"Speaking of my father and grandfather..." Leighton muttered, suddenly turning solemn. "They're the reason you were ever in this whole mess in the first place. They were jealous of your birth pack's high prestige ranking, so they took one of our elder's advice and kidnapped you. They thought it would bring great gain to the pack and finally give it the upper hand they needed to be viewed as more powerful than your true pack.

"I've never told you this, but they've been keeping my true mate hostage for the past three years. When I first found her, I had no ideas of their plans. I had just turned 16 and stumbled upon her during one of my patrol routes. I'd never been so happy in my entire life." He said, voice cracking from emotion towards the end.

Tears gathered in my eyes as I wished I could comfort one of my closest friends.

"I immediately brought her home. I never understood why my mom begged me to turn her away and hide her before my father found out. I thought that she didn't view her as worth enough for me. Turns out, she only ever wanted me to be happy and wanted to keep us both from getting hurt. I was young and dumb, and I refused my mother's wishes. My father came home later that night. He flipped out on me when I told him my news. Before I even knew what was going on, I was being restrained with silver and she was being dragged away. I don't even know where they're holding her, Aceso." He whimpered, finally breaking down. Tears slid down his cheeks as he sobbed for his snatched mate.

I couldn't keep in my hysteric cries as I buried my face into Xavier's chest. He rubbed his hand up and down my neck, trying to comfort me, but nothing was working. How could any rational human being ever do this to someone they're supposed to love?

"You need to calm down, love. You're going to make yourself sick and it isn't good for the baby." Xavier said, trying to calm me down while being the only rational one between the two of us. I nodded while trying to take deep breaths to calm my raggedly beating heart.

"We have to help him!" I pleaded to Xavier with both my words and eyes. To my surprise, he actually nodded in agreeance with me and pull out a what I assumed to be a master key because there was only one of the chain.

"You may take residence in our pack and we will help you in every way that we can. The retired Alpha and I have already been working on some plans of attack for you old pack, and if you'd like to join us, you may. We could use your insider knowledge of the pack as an advantage." He said while letting Leighton out of the cell.

I guffawed at him, "You are actually offering him a place to stay and not only inviting him to view your war plans, but you're offering him a position to help? Who are you, and what have you done to my mate?" I said, feigning suspicion.

"You're forgetting that I know what it's like to be without my mate. It's agonizing, but to have met your met and then be without them... I can't even imagine what you've been through. You have my condolences and also my word that I will do everything in my power to help you find her." He spoke with such conviction. The fierceness in his eyes, and how thoughtful he way being, was such a turn on. The scent of my arousal permeated the air thickly, and I could tell the minute both men registered it. Leighton scrunched his nose up in distaste and Xavier's eyes went pitch black with lust.

"Yuck, newly mates are disgusting. Get a room." Leighton muttered before walking a few feet ahead of us. "Let's go!" He said, visibly breathing through his nose. I laughed as his discomfort before beginning to walk towards him. Xavier's hand reached down to cup my ass while we walked, letting me know where his thoughts were.

"Later." I mumbled in response. He released an annoyed, but husky growl before nodding.

After getting Leighton something to eat and letting him shower and change his clothes, we were all crammed in Xavier's office along with the higher ranks and head pack warriors. There were maps sprawled everywhere, along with random notes here and there that were gathered by border patrol about Nightshade's security rounds. It took some time for Xavier and everyone else involved to fully explain the plan to not only Leighton, but me as well. I'd been left out of the loop of information up until this point. Xavier wanted to keep it that way, but I refused to leave and he knew not to push me on it.

I have to admit, the plan was flawless. It could be because I have absolutely zero experience when it comes to all things military and such, but it seemed like they had ironed out every last detail. Even Leighton agreed.

"Fuck. We had no chance, did we?" He said through a chuckle of disbelief.

"Not really, no." Xavier replied smugly.

"I can tell you one thing you won't want to do though. There's a plot of land here," he said pointing to a particular area on the map, "that he has on the highest maximum security possible. It's an awkward plot of secluded land, and though he makes it appear as if there's nothing there, his security measures say otherwise." Leighton said, his eyebrows scrunched in confusion. Xavier nodded his head, looking deep in thought.

"Not to be a huge dick, but did you ever think that that might be where he's keeping your mate?" Xavier asked in a 'duh' tone. Leighton seemed to contemplate it for a second before leaning back against his chair and scoffing.

"Fucking hell. She's been right under my nose the whole time and I never even suspected. No wonder he always warned to beat me if I ever explored that land." He said, shaking his head at his own stupidity.

"He probably knew that as soon as you found her, you'd run away and spill all his dirty little secrets and ruin his plans." I said, putting in my own two-sense.

"That's exactly what was going on." Xavier agreed.

"If he knows I've escaped and headed straight for this territory, which he I have no doubt he does, then there's nothing stopping him from hurting my love. Whatever time you were thinking of executing these plans needs to be moved up to, like, yesterday." Leighton stated, looking extremely stressed.

"Not happening." Xavier replied instantly. "Our warriors are nowhere near ready for this kind of battle. We need at least a solid three more weeks, otherwise my people will get hurt and I won't stand for that." He said with finality. I admired that he was always looking out for everyone's best interest.

"He'll kill her before the week is over!" Leighton yelled back, clearly panicking.

"It'll be okay. We formulate a plan to get her before the main attack plan. We'll just need to figure out a way to infiltrate their territory without alerting them right away so we can get her and escape before they have time to retaliate." I reasoned while rubbing soothing circles into his back. He nodded, but looked like he didn't have enough energy to continue the conversation.

"Leighton, get some rest. Tomorrow morning you and I can discuss your mate's rescue. For now, there is nothing we can do but pray for her safety." Xavier said before dismissing the meeting.

It was a few hours later and I was livid. Xavier left the mother fucking seat on the toilet up again – even thought I've asked him a million and one times to put it down when he's done – and I ended up falling in. The minor annoyance would have been something you simply brush off with a few curse words, but these pregnancy hormones were a bitch. After fuming over the fact that he never listens to my pleas for him to put the seat down for a good twenty minutes, I began thinking about how he lied to me about the pregnancy again, which then led me to get mad at myself for letting him off the hook so easily yesterday.

He was walking right into a shit storm and he didn't even know it.

He wandered into the room, looking tired and annoyed. Too fucking bad.

"Hi baby." He greeted me while leaning down to try and kiss me. I growled at him before turning my head to the side so his lips hit my cheek.

"What the-?" He started but I cut him off.

"Don't 'baby' me asshole. It's all your fault that you sweet talked me out of being angry yesterday. You never listen to me!" I yelled, stomping my foot like a five year old. He blinked a few times, the look of confusion not fading for even a second.

"So you're angry at me for talking you out of being angry? Or you're angry at me for not listening?" He asked, sounding genuinely lost.

"NO!" I screeched. "I'm mad at you for...for...both! Neither! I don't know!" I yelled, pushing him away from me with my hands and turning on my heels to head into the closet.

"Wait, what?" He questioned, following my every footstep.

"Just go! I don't want you in here tonight!" I sobbed, throwing clothes around while looking for my favorite nightshirt – which just so happened to be Xavier's.

"No. This is our room and after the long day I've had I just want to hold you while I sleep." She said sternly.

"Just get everything you need and go!" I stated, back still turned to him. I heard fading sound of footsteps, so I assumed he was leaving. Once I finally changed, I reentered the bedroom, only to see Xavier crawling into bed, naked.

"I thought I told you to get everything you needed and go." I snapped, crossing my arms over my chest.

"And I told you that I wasn't sleeping elsewhere. This is our room and this is our bed and I have every intention of sleeping in it with you." He spoke with emphasis.

"No. You obviously don't respect my wishes or the promise that we made to each other the first night we met. Or did you already forget that?" I mocked, tears already beginning to resurface.

"Why are you back on this? We've had this conversation already, Aceso!" He retorted back.

I didn't say anything in return, rather just stood there upset. I hugged myself while silently crying. I heard the rustling of sheets and was soon being pulled into Xavier's strong, warm embrace.

"Baby, don't cry." He pleaded, placing gentle pecks against my skin.

"They won't fucking stop!" I whined, wiping my tears away furiously. "You don't even u-understand how fucking annoying it is t-to never be in control of your emotions!" I yelled.

He chuckled quietly, "I'm sorry, pretty girl. How about I rub your feet until you fall asleep?" He murmured against my skin.

I groaned, "Dear god that sounds so good. Yes please." In the midst of rubbing my arches I mumbled, "Oh, by the way, we have another ultrasound in two weeks." His eyes lit up and a smile from ear to ear appeared on his face. It was the perfect site to be engrained in my brain right before slipping into a blissful sleep.

Chapter 20

ceso's POV

A   I would like to say the last two weeks have flown by, but that would be a bald-faced lie. Xavier's been hovering around me 24/7 – even worse than before, which I never thought to be possible. He almost tried to tell me I wasn't allowed to walk down the stairs on my own and that I had to be carried. That conversation went real well.

"Would you please stop pacing, Xav? It'll be fine!" I tried reasoning. He's been jittery ever since we went to bed last night. Having not been at the first ultrasound, he doesn't know what to expect and it's making him anxious and jumpy.

"How about we leave now? We don't want to be late, baby." He said, pleading me with his eyes. I restrained from rolling my own at his ridiculousness.

"Xavier, babe, our appointment isn't for another 30 minutes and it's only a five minute walk to the doctor's office from here." I spoke slowly, trying to get it through his thick skull. I knew it was no use though. If he wanted to go now, he was going to make it happen. Blushing in response to my words, he nodded.

"I'm just excited is all. I didn't get to be at the first one so while you've already gotten the experience of seeing our child, I haven't." He said, bringing his hand up to rest against my belly protectively. Guilt ate away at my insides from his words. Of course I'm not happy that I did what I did, but damn it! I was pissed at him and I wasn't thinking straight. "Stop that. It's not your fault your hormones got the best of you. These things happen." He said with conviction, having sensed my internal battle.

"Why don't we head over now and see if she's ready early?" I suggested, knowing he doesn't want to wait another second. A breathtaking smile overtook his face. Standing up, he swooped me into his arms and kissed my cheek. I giggled to myself as he carried me, bridal style, all the way to the doctors.

"Look at you! You're already noticeably showing!" The doctor commented as we walked into the examination room. I laughed and nodded in agreement, rubbing my tummy in soothing circles. "Alright, well lets get this thing going, shall we?" She asked, looking back and forth between Xavier and I. After Xavier refusing to let me hop up onto the table, and instead lifting me up himself, we were finally able to get the fun part of the appointment started.

"Alright, Ms. Luna, same procedure as last time. Here comes the cold gel." She said, giving me a forewarning, unlike the last time. Soon, there was the same white, pixilated image displayed on the screen. The only difference was that this time around it was a slightly bigger and more noticeable.

"There's your baby!" The doctor said with excitement while pointing at the computer monitor.

"It's developing perfectly! Would you like to hear the heartbeat?" She asked, looking directly at Xavier.

"Yes, please." He answered immediately, sounding a little breathless. Seconds later a loud whooshing noise filled the room. I gripped Xavier's hand that was holding mine hard as I watched tears well up in his eyes. One slipped out and began to cascade down his cheek, but I wiped it away before it got too far.

"I never thought I'd get to experience this...thank you." He whispered against my lips before kissing me soundly, the salty taste of his tears mixing with his familiar peppermint one.

"You don't need to thank me. I'm just as lucky to have an amazing mate like you." I mumbled, leaning my forehead against his. I heard a throat clear next to me and backed away from Xavier, embarrassed that the doctor saw our intimate moment of affection.

"Anyway, I've printed out your due date on the ultrasound picture, which is right here." She said, extending her hand to give me the print out. I dozed off as the pack doctor spent the next 30 minutes explaining how werewolf pregnancies work to Xavier. I must have fallen asleep because the next thing I knew, I woke up on the couch in Xavier's office as he worked away soundlessly.

"Good evening sleeping beauty." Xavier teased when he realized I'd come to.

"How long have I been out?" I asked, voice raspy from sleep.

"About two, three hours maybe? You haven't missed much." He said while abandoning whatever he was working on to come sit next to me.

"I'm still exhausted." I said while rubbing my hands over my face roughly.

"That's cause my boy's taking it all from you!" He said cheekily. I scoffed at his confidence.

"And how do you know it's a boy?" I challenged.

"It's a Campbell men thing. Our mates never birth anything but males the first time. There're very few women in our lineage, and it goes back hundreds of generations. Though, I would love to have a little girl. One that looks just like her beautiful mother." He trailed off, looking deep in thought before winking at me.

"We'll see about that." I muttered sleepily.

"Also, I'll be leaving tonight at eight for Nightshade. We've concluded now is the best time to get Leighton's mate." He said with annoyance. My body tensed up immediately at his words.

"And just what does this mission entail?" I questioned. If anything happened to him, I'd never make it.

"C'mon, baby. You know I'll be careful." He said, trying to smooth my ruffled feathers.

"What is your plan, Xavier?" I bit out, wanting to know exactly what he was blindly getting himself into.

He sighed deeply. "We think we've located exactly where Alpha Jack is keeping Leighton's mate. We know warriors secure the land 24/7, but we aren't sure what else is protecting that plot of land. I'm taking 30 of my best men, but only ten are going to be with me. Jack thinks we're coming on behalf of a new border treaty, but while we're discussing that, Leighton and my 20 other men will be sneaking their way onto the secured plot of land and figuring out if our suspicions are right."

I mulled over what he'd just told me. It didn't sound dangerous, but anything could go wrong. Horribly wrong. Alpha Jack was a demented, sick man and I didn't want Xavier anywhere near him or his corrupt pack.

"I'm going with you." I stated, not leaving any room for discussion.

"Fuck no you're not. I'm not arguing with you about this, Aceso. There's no reason for you to be on Nightshade territory. I'm placing the pack in lockdown while we're gone just in case anything was to happen, and that lockdown includes you. You will be staying in the underground cellar with all the women and children." I growled at him, wanting to argue, but I knew there was no use. I wasn't going on this mission with him and he's made sure of it.

Xavier's POV

Riding in the car was never a favorite pastime of mine, especially when it came to gravel roads. I hated being jostled around - it made me nauseous. Either it was that, or having to be away from Aceso. I'm thinking more of the latter, but I didn't want to dwell on that right now. I needed to focus on the task at hand, and that was ridding Alpha Jack of any leverage he had over his son.

Fucking prick.

"How you feeling, man?" Beta Aaron asked quietly.

"Annoyed. I fucking hate this bastard." I growled out. Aaron nodded in agreement before turning his gaze back to the road.

"She'll be fine, dude. You made her promise to stay in the cellar and there's God knows how many guards surrounding every entrance." He spoke, knowing exactly what I was worrying about.

"It doesn't feel like enough." I mumbled.

"It never does, trust me." He scoffed, shaking his head from what I believed to be a past memory.

The closer we get to the border, the tenser my body became. I hated being on land that wasn't my own. There's nothing worse than fighting blind and being at a disadvantage.

Calm down, Sweetheart. I know you're worried, but you shouldn't be. I'm still locked up in this damn cellar with my mom and sister. You should be proud they've managed to keep me down here so long. Aceso grumbled at me through the mind link. She must have sensed my mild distress. What would I do without her?

I chuckled at her words before replying. I know baby girl, but I can't trust anybody with you. Not after waiting for you for so long. I hate that I can't be there to protect you.

Before I could hear her reply, the card came to an abrupt halt.

"We're here..." Aaron muttered to everyone in the car. I clenched my fists and jaw, taking a deep breath to calm myself before getting out. As I walked closer to the front of the pack house, Alpha Jack's large frame became more noticeable. He stood with his arms crossed, standing in front of the entrance to his pack house.

"Welcome to my pack, Alpha Xavier." He bit out, looking about as happy as I currently was. I continued to look him over, realizing how disheveled he really looked.

"Did something happen, Jack? You don't look well." I commented, purposely trying to rile him up. I could see him grinding his teeth at my remark and couldn't help but smirk.

"You'll have to excuse me, my son has gone missing and we believe he's been taken by rogues for some unknown reason." He said, lying through his teeth. If only he knew that his son was currently working with my men to royally fuck him over. This caused my smirk to grow. He must have noticed because he narrowed his eyes at me before glaring.

"Why don't we go to your office and discuss the terms of the new border line, yes?" I asked before he had the chance to question my intentions. He grunted in response before turning around and leading me, and the rest of my men, to his office. He was completely unsuspecting of what was happening behind his back right about now.

I snapped my fingers the second we entered Jack's office. My top warriors abruptly grabbed Alpha Jack, catching him off guard, and held him down while slipping a pair of silver handcuffs around his wrists. Jarrod turned and locked the office doors, ensuring no one came in or went out while. My face turned deadly as I glared at the man I hated more than the devil himself.

"You're such a pathetic fucking excuse for an Alpha, you know that Jack?" I growled. "To think you could steal a child right out from under the parents' nose, and then actually get away with it? Disgusting!" I spat, my anger only increasing. I watched as his eyes widened, obviously not expecting us to find out about his little indiscretions.

"I know you've heard about my reputation Jack. I know you knew not to fuck with what was mine, but you did anyway, didn't you? Now, you're going to find out exactly what I do to those that double cross me." I growled out, extending my claws and glaring at him maliciously.

Chapter 21

Xavier's POV

Just as I begin to make my ascent towards him to deliver the punishment he rightfully deserves, he begins laughing like a mad man. I stop in my tracks and glance at him wearily.

"Did you really think I was that fucking stupid, Alpha Xavier? I knew my pathetic excuse for a son ran right to your pack the second he crossed our borders. I also knew that you'd help him, because you've become quite the little bitch ever since you mated. In case you're wondering, my son and your warriors are heading right into a death trap, and it will be entirely your fault. Let that sit on your conscious." He spat while smiling at me. He's fucking crazy I thought to myself. Then his words fully registered in my mind. Fuck!

Fuck, fuck, fuck, fuck! My men are going to die because of my stupidity!

"Lets go!" I yelled, tearing the door off its hinges and sprinting through the pack house. I somehow managed to find my way to the backdoor and into the backwoods. I could hear everyone trailing behind me, so I shifted and continued to run as fast as I could.

Aaron! Aaron it's a trap! Don't go any further! I yelled through the mind link, but I was met with silence. This isn't good. This isn't good at all.

Aaron? Leighton? No one was answering. It was almost as if they were purposely blocking me out. I pushed harder, trying my best to sniff out their scent. I only had a slight idea concerning where I was going because I was on totally unfamiliar land. I caught the faintest smell of wolfsbane gas and skidded to a halt. That mother fucker...

That asshole gassed them. We need to get them out, and alive. The gas won't take full effect unless you've breathed it in for half an hour or more, so we need to work quickly. If anyone who isn't one of us gets in your way, kill them quickly. Lets go. I instructed those with me before diving headfirst into the faint cloud of gas surrounding the area.

My eyes began to burn and blur, making it hard to see the wolf coming at me until he was nearly right in front of me. He tackled me, aiming for my neck instantly. I was able to shift my weight enough to flip him and rip his throat out before he was able to grab at mine again. I sneezed, trying to get the wolfsbane out of my nose. Fuck, this shit is horrible. I whimpered when I saw one of my men a few feet ahead of me, dead. It wasn't supposed to be like this.

15 minutes later, and we had the situation almost under control, but Leighton, nor any of my 20 other men, were to be seen. I glanced around frantically, looking for a clue. Anything as to insight on where they went or what happened to them.

I finally spotted a raised chunk of the forest floor and ran to investigate it. I shifted back quickly, trying to hold my breath for as long as I could while I roamed my hands over the ground hurriedly. I finally caught a lip in the ground and yanked up, revealing a trap door of sorts.

"C'mon! In the ground!" I yelled out to my remaining men. We all jumped down before I shut the hatch quickly, taking in deep lungfuls of clean air.

"What now, Alpha?" One of my men asked. I coughed, hacking up black gunk. Fixing whatever the fuck that was would have to come later.

"Spread out. Two go in each direction. Meet back here in ten minutes, regardless if you find something or not. I'm not losing another man to this bastard pack." I growled out. They all nodded before scurrying off. I rubbed my face, thinking about the fact that we left Alpha jack completely unattended. Granted he was still cuffed and didn't have the key, I knew he was a man of resources. He's made that much obvious.

I made my way through the intricately designed cells, doing my best to remain quiet and unseen. Leighton said the plot of land was guarded, but he never said if the actual cells were too. I wouldn't put it past Jack to get cocky and think no one would ever make it this far.

"You piece of shit! I hope you rot in fucking hell! You were a worthless excuse for a Beta! When I get my hands on the Alpha title, I'll rid this fucking world of you and every other corrupt leader!" I heard someone yell. I instantly recognized the voice as belonging to Leighton and quickly headed in that direction. I crept up before peeking around the corner. Who

I assumed was Jack's Beta was standing in front of a cell that contained Leighton's beat up and bleeding form. His arms were crossed and his face held a stoic expression at Leighton yelled at him.

"That'll never happen kid and you fucking know it. Your daddy will shoot you dead before you even see that title. Filthy mutt." He spat before turning to leave. I sprang out, snapping his neck in seconds and releasing his body. It hit the ground with a loud thump. I kicked it as I stepped over it.

"Where are the keys?" I asked Leighton gruffly.

"Thank god you're here. I think they're in his pocket." He said, jutting his head out towards the Beta I just killed. Rummaging around in his pockets, I eventually found them and let him out.

"Did you find your mate?" I asked while stripping the Beta of his jeans. I didn't want to continue walking around stark naked. Especially when I had plans of being in the presence of a female who wasn't my mate.

"I think she's in quartile six, whatever that means. I heard one of the guards mumbling it while they were doing their border rounds outside." He said, looking deep in thought. We walked for a few more minutes until we met up with the group.

"Do you know where quartile six could be? The construction of this place was well thought out." I said, the compliment burning as I spoke it.

"Did you say six?" One of my men mumbled, his attention peaking.

"Yes. What do you know?" I demanded.

"I came to an entrance with the number 6 painted on the wall. It's worth a shot." He said firmly. A feeling of pride flourished in my chest. I had trained these men well.

"Lead the way." I ordered.

Ten minutes later, we came upon a dark, dingy hallway.

"Help. Help me. Somebody...please. Help." The cries for help were so faint you almost couldn't hear them. They were quiet and sounded exhausted, raspy.

"That has to be her!" Leighton yelled, rushing down the hallway. He frantically searched the cells left and right before he abruptly stopped in front of one.

"Love? Love can you hear me? Look at me! I need you to move, okay? Go to the back of the cell. C'mon, you can do it! I know you can!" Leighton began, trying to coax his mate in the cell to listen.

"There you go, good girl. Now turn your face, okay? Good." He stepped back before beginning to violently kick at the bars. There wasn't any way for him to touch them with his bare skin without receiving third degree burns from the silver. We all stayed back, knowing that we would be more of a hindrance than help with how small the hall way space was. Finally after minutes of him kicking as hard as he could, the bars began to give.

"Look baby! Come here, look. You can crawl through. Come one. You can do it!" He yelled. The body that began to crawl through the space he made looked horrible. It was nothing but skin and bones. Her hair was stringy and matted to her face and body with no only dirt, but also blood. She was a small, frail thing. Her head, unable to be supported by her weak head, lolled back and Leighton picked her up bridal style and began to carry her. My heart stopped beating for a millisecond before I abruptly turned and began walking again.

"Let's go. There's going to be an ambush waiting for us at the doors. Unless, Jack is stupid." I said over my shoulder.

I counted to three before pushing the escape door open quickly. I jumped out, crouched and ready to fight but the land was dead. There wasn't a soul in sight. I listened intently for a few minutes before concluding that there wasn't any-one within a five-mile radius.

"Lets go, there's no one here. She needs medical attention, and now."

Aceso's POV

I paced the cellar anxiously, rubbing my stomach to try and soothe it. Having severe morning sickness while being cooped up in a small room with a hoard of people wasn't exactly ideal. Not to mention, my nerves were through the roof with Xavier being gone.

"Sweetheart, you're going to make yourself sicker than you already are. Sit down." My mom said while patting the space next to her on the couch.

"I can't. Xavier could be hurt and I wouldn't even know it!" I whined.

"Hush. You know that isn't true. You would feel his pain. Relax, you need to think about your baby." My mother said, harsher than before. Suddenly, the sound of the front door slamming captured everyone's attention. I breathed deeply, Xavier's earthy smell enveloping my senses. I pushed through the crowd and dashed passed my enforcers, heading to where I could smell my mate. The sight of him nearly brought me to tears. I jumped at him the second I was close enough, engulfing him into a tight hug. I frantically ran my hands over his body, making sure there wasn't a single scratch or cut on him. I glance up at his face to see him staring ahead, blankly. I became worried instantly. His eyes were glazed over and he was breathing rapidly, letting me know that he was in some sort of state of shock.

"Xavier, baby? Talk to me. What's wrong? What happened?" I said, shooting question after question at him. He looked down, eyes widening as if noticing me standing there for the first time. His grip on me tightened as if to reassure that I was actually there and he wasn't hallucinating.

"My...my sister is alive." He rasped out before breaking down into hysterics.

Chapter 22

Aceso's POV

I didn't know what to say. I was totally, and utterly speechless for two significant reasons.

One, Xavier never mentioned anything about having a sister.

And two, I've only ever seen Xavier shed a few tears on one other occasion and that was during our doctor's appoint just a few weeks ago. But this wasn't one or two tears, oh no, this was full on sobs. It was heartbreaking. No, more like shattering.

My wolf growled at me in the back of my mind and I immediately jolted out of my state of shock and pulled Xavier's head into the crevice between my neck and shoulder. I ran my hands soothingly from his head to the top of his back, murmuring words here and there to comfort him.

"Lets go to our room, okay?" I whispered against his ear. His body continued to shudder from his deep heaves, but I was able to feel the slight movement of his head nodding up and down in agreement.

After guiding him up the stairs, into our room, and towards the edge of our bed, I finally asked him the question that'd been right on the tip of my tongue.

"I thought you said only you and 12 other men survived the attack?" I asked, cupping his cheeks between my hands and gently rubbing my fingers over his smooth skin, loving the slight roughness and resistance that his stubble gave against my fingers.

"So did I. It's her. I know it's her, Aceso." He rasped out, a fresh wave of tears spilling from his red, bloodshot eyes. I wiped the wet tracks away before speaking.

"I know, baby. I believe you, but why didn't you tell me about her before? You told me all about your family but you never once mentioned her." I said, a little hurt that he wasn't completely honest with me when he said he was an only child.

"After the accident, I told myself I never had a sister. I chose to forget all about her because it hurt so bad to think about. That I wasn't able to protect my little sister, who looked up to me and depended on me and put her faith in me. It tore me apart, Aceso." He said, a slight whimper to his voice.

"Don't," I scolded giving him a harsh look, "don't do that to yourself. I know for a fact that you gave your all to keep the ones you loved safe. You're the most compassionate, amazing man I've ever met and I don't doubt for a second that you tried your best to keep her safe." I said fiercely, leaving no room for argument. He leaned down, because even sitting down with me in between his legs he was still taller than me, and kissed me deeply while pulling me closer to his body.

"She forgot about me..." He said, voice no louder than a whisper.

"What?" I asked. My brows furrowed in confusion.

"She looked right at me and didn't recognize me at all. She had no idea who I was." He muttered, looking utterly broken. My inner wolf whined so loud I flinched.

"That's ridiculous, Xavier. She's been through a lot, you both have. Give her some time before you try and talk about what happened, okay? Lie down and get some rest. I'm gonna go make you some food. I'll bring it up when I'm done." I instructed before pecking his lips and beginning to make my way down stairs.

I entered the kitchen to see a freshly showered and clothed Leighton, as well as his mate seated right next to him nibbling on a small peanut butter and jelly sandwich.

Neither of them were aware of my presence just yet. Xavier's sister, whose name I've yet to learn, was totally focused on the food in her hands while Leighton was busy watching her eat. I took that moment to get a good look at her. Her and Xavier's similarities were more than obvious. They had beautiful eyes and hair as well as naturally golden skin. How she managed that while being locked inside of a cell I don't know. Though she was clearly underweight from not being fed regularly, I could tell she was absolutely stunning just like her brother.

I cleared my throat so that I didn't completely startle them when they saw me. The quite sound caused Leighton's mate to shoot up in shock and then cower before she realized who it was that made the noise. Her reaction caused Leighton to instinctively turn and growl at me before he realized what he was doing and muttered a quick sorry.

"I was just making some food. Don't mind me." I said gently before getting out all the ingredients I needed to make grilled cheese with tomato soup.

"What's your name?" I hear a small, mouse like voice ask. I turned and smiled at her before replying.

"Aceso, how about you?" I spoke quietly as to not scare her.

"Charlotte." She mumbled to which I nodded.

"That's a beautiful name." I complimented before working up the courage to ask the question I really wanted to. "How have you been holding up?" I asked, hoping it wasn't too invasive.

"I'm doing better. The wolfsbane is almost out of my system and I'm starting to remember things again." She said on a sigh. Like a light bulb going off in my head, I realized something that Xavier hadn't.

"You've been completely out of it up until now, huh?" I sympathized.

She nodded meekly. "Pretty much."

"Well, if you're up to it, there's something that I think you need to meet." I said, glancing at Leighton for his okay. He nodded, knowing as well as I did that she needed this. They both needed this. My words seemed to cause her slight distress, but Leighton rested his hand against the small of her back and began rubbing in circles. She nodded and hopped off the stool with a slight assistance from Leighton.

Plating the two grilled cheeses I made, I handed Leighton the bowl of soup before motioning for them to follow me.

Our footsteps were quiet as we reached Xavier and I's door on the second floor. I gave Charlotte one last look before pushing the door open and entering. I set the food down on the dresser and cleared my throat, getting Xavier's attention from where he was sitting on the edge of the bed with his head in his hands. He looked up and gazed at me before adverting his eyes to the two figures looming behind me.

I hear a quick intake of breath from behind me and step out of the way.

"Oh my god!" Charlotte breathed out before bursting into tears. Xavier stood from the edge of the bed and captured Charlotte in a tight embrace as she ran and crashed into him. Her cries were loud and sorrowful as she soaked Xavier's shirt with her tears.

"I was so scared bubba! I was so scared!" She cried against his chest, tightening her grip on his shirt material between her fingers. Her cries turned hysterical as he continued to murmur about how sorry he was over and over. I struggled to keep my tears at bay as I watched the scene unfold before me.

"What happened to you Charlie? I thought you were dead!" Xavier gritted out, voice thick with emotion.

"God, there was so much happening all at once. It was like everything was totally fine and then it just... wasn't. They'd already killed dad, and mom was screaming at me to run. I didn't know where I was supposed to run, I was 14 and had never been alone like that before. I just started running. I didn't know I was heading for anyone's territory until I had already crossed it. I thought I was going to be okay when I found Leighton, but that's when we both found out exactly what his dad's plan was. I've been locked up for three years." She rasped out, her tears never once stopping. I could tell by the way Xavier's jaw was clenching and the glares he kept throwing that he wanted to hurt Leighton, but knew it would be illogical because Leighton was a victim in this situation, just like his sister was.

"What about you, bubba? What happened?" She finally asked once her tears had begun to subside. Xavier pulled down to sit next to him while beckoning for me to come to him. I pushed myself off the doorframe and made my way over, listening to him recap how he handled the situation once they'd finished off every last rogue.

"I can't believe you had to go through all of that alone. I'm so sorry." She wept. "Mom and dad...are they...did they get buried?" She asked timidly, appearing afraid of what answer Xavier was about to give her.

"Of course, Charlie! We managed to give them, and all other wolf remains we could find, a proper burial. Once this war is over, we can go back and visit their graves. I promise." Xavier reassured her. She breathed a sigh of relief. I felt so bad for her. Being 17 and having not a single parent left would be devastating.

My stomach rumbled, but the thought of grilled cheese repulsed me.

"I'm going to go make some hot cocoa and something to eat, I'll be right back" I said, knowing if I didn't go get the food myself Xavier would wander back up here with a weeks worth of food.

Wandering into the kitchen I began raiding the cabinets, fridge, and freezer for anything that sounded even remotely appealing. Having no luck, I settled for making the hot chocolate first. Grabbing out the milk from the fridge, I turned back around, only to be faced with my worst nightmare. I screamed at the top of my lungs before I was slapped across the face. This wasn't going to end well.

Chapter 23

Aceso's POV

My ear-piercing scream was cut short by a harsh slap across my face. My cheek stung as tears gathered in my eyes.

"Shut the fuck up or I'll blow your fucking brains all over this god damn kitchen! You hear me?" Alpha Jack growled menacingly in my face. I scanned his features and grew more scared then I ever have been in my entire life. He's gone crazy.

I sobbed as I realized there's a large possibility I wasn't making it out of this situation alive. I almost didn't catch the sound of pounding footsteps coming towards the kitchen because of my own tears.

Jack must have heard the footsteps as well, because he suddenly flipped our positions. He pulled my body in front of his own, grasping my neck tightly in his hand, pressing his thumb against my windpipe and making it difficult to breathe. Xavier came running into the room first, face loosing all color when he saw the situation I was in. Jack suddenly pulled out a gun and pressed the cold metal tip to my slightly protruding stomach.

"No! God, please no!" I screamed through panicked hiccups.

"Take one more step and it's bye-bye to your first born, Xavier." Jack sneered in a menacing tone laced with amusement. He was truly a sick bastard. Xavier lifted his hands into the air in a surrendering motion before standing rooted in his spot. Leighton and Charlotte soon entered the room, both their eyes growing wide with terror at the sight before them.

"P-please. D-don't hurt my baby!" I begged, knees beginning to buckle as the weight of the situation dawned on me.

"Shut up! All of you shut up!" He screamed moving his hand away from my stomach to waver it back and forth between the others in the room. If I weren't terrified for my life, I would laugh at how idiotic he was being. No one was even speaking but me.

"You're all going to shut the fuck up while I talk. Anyone that interrupts gets a bullet between their eyes." He said eerily calm, but I could tell he was still loosing it by the subtle shake of his hands.

"You can't even imagine the childhood I had growing up. My father never cared about anything but being the best. He always had to be the best at everything. If I weren't meeting his expectations, no matter what it was, I would be beaten. Some days, I couldn't get out of bed because he'd been merciless. He trained me to be a ruthless Alpha like himself since the day I came out of the womb. 'Pain is for pussies!' he would say. 'Never show any emotion but anger. Be unforgiving and hard. No one likes a bitch Alpha!' Everyday! It was drilled into my brain for 25 God damn years!" He paused his story to gather his thoughts. His breathing was ragged and quick and I swallowed the lump in my throat.

"It only got worse after this stupid bitch and her sister were born!" He screeched, momentarily tightening his grip on my throat and blocking my airway completely. Xavier's roar caused his grip to loosen and I immediately gulped in large breaths of air before coughing harshly.

"So, we came up with the plan. It was going to change everything. We were going to be a family again. We were going to be the pack on top again. But then you came into the picture!" He spat, pointing his gun and aiming at Xavier's head. My body tensed immediately as I repeatedly chanted a prayer to the Moon Goddess over and over for her to keep him safe.

"I'm fucking done being second place to this shitty fucking pack!" Alpha Jack suddenly yelled. It seemed like it all happened in two seconds. He flicked the safety off before turning the gun back on my stomach. I shut my eyes, but I refused to stay still. I wouldn't let him take my baby from me without a fight. I would give my life for my child. I could hear movement happening around me, but my mind had already shut down. Xavier's familiar growl echoed around the room. I peeked my eyes open just in time to see Xavier lung for both Jack and I. Xavier managed to nudge Jack's arm, but it just wasn't enough.

All commotion in the room ceased after the telltale deafening pop of a gunshot rang throughout room. Pain ricocheted all over my body, waking me up from the numb mindset I'd been in. Looking down, I realized that instead of Xavier knocking the gun out of Jack's hand completely, he threw off Jack's aim. Blood flowed in an endless stream from my chest, a few inches from my heart. My mind went fuzzy and I couldn't hold my own weight anymore. I looked up, the last thing I saw before my eyes rolled into the back of my head was Xavier's mouth moving in silent screams as he reached for me.

I began to come to my senses. Everything felt warm and fuzzy and there was a golden light casting over everything. I released a content sigh as the warmth wrapped around my skin, caressing me sweetly like the touch of your lover. I'd never felt this safe before. Everything just seemed so...right.

I reached down to rest my hand upon my stomach, relaxing instantly when my hand came in contact with my perfect little bump. I patted it lightly, smiling happily to myself.

I jolted upright at the sound of a giggle in the distance. My heart began to race as the peaceful atmosphere was abruptly interrupted. I turned and came face to face with two absolutely stunning women. They resembled Alethia and I, but their facial structures were slightly different. They were wearing long, beautiful white silk dresses that trailed behind them as they approached me, hand in hand.

"Hello there, sweet Luna." The brunette spoke, shattering the silence. Her voice was soft, but strong and I detected traces of power amongst her being. Though I had no idea who this stranger was, I wasn't scared by her presence at all, just curious.

"W-who are you!" I replied, holding her stomach protectively while baring my canines. I may not feel threatened by them, but I refused to be tricked. For all I know, this could be a trap. It was then that I suddenly realized I had no idea where I was, or what time it was.

"Calm down, Sweetpea! We pose no threat! We have only come bearing advice and love." The blonde assured me, her voice serving to smooth my ruffled feathers.

"You've done a wonderful job so far as the healer. There's been much more action since I've handed the job down, that's for sure." The blonde giggles out. I gasped in realization as her words registered in my mind. These two women must be the past healer and peacekeeper wolves that died when Aceso and I were born. But if that's true then...

"Oh my god! I'm dead." I cried. "Xavier! No! God no, please I need to be with Xavier!" I screamed hysterically, tears springing to my eyes instantly as a feeling of regret settled in the pit of my stomach. The eyes of the two in front of me grew and they rushed towards me.

"No! Calm down, you're okay! You're not dead, silly!" The peacekeeper said, trying to calm my erratic breathing. "You're in a coma. You have been for quite a while now. We've come to tell you that it's time you go back. Our kind needs you. Your mate needs you. And..." She said, trailing off. I was about to yell at her to cut the shit and finish her sentence, but then I suddenly heard the little pitter patter of feet coming towards us. A child, no older than two, peeked out from behind the two women while sucking on his thumb.

Upon seeing me, he pulled his thumb from his mouth as a wide grin set upon his face. "Momma!" He screeched before running towards me, with slight difficulty, and hitting me head on. His arms wrapped around my leg as his little baby legs struggled to keep his body upright.

"He needs you." The peacekeeper murmured, finishing her previous sentence. I couldn't control my tears as I scanned the face of the little boy. My son. God, he was the spitting image of Xavier, but with my eyes. I couldn't believe what I was seeing and experiencing. I leaned down and hoisted him upon my hip, running my fingers across his pudgy cheeks. I was so in love. After I remembered what she'd said to me earlier, a wave of anger hit me.

"What are you talking about? Why would I be here if I had a choice in the matter!" I yelled, letting my anger get the best of me and shouting at her. I was pissed that she was acting as if it was my fault I was still stuck here in coma land.

"That's just it. Until you were ready to face the world after your...experience, you stayed here without consciousness. You'd still be there had it not been for our help. It's not natural for the healer wolf to get hurt. Actually, I don't think it's ever happened. Oh, how you worried the Moon Goddess so!" The blonde exclaimed sporting an extremely distressed scowl.

"We mustn't waste more time. We shall be watching over you, Aceso. Always." They whispered simultaneously before grabbing the little boy from my arms and simultaneously kissing me on each cheek. They brought their hands up before abruptly shoving me back harshly. I released a scream, expecting to hit the ground, but I just kept falling.

My eyes fluttered open in fright, but I instantly regretted it. The bright, white light was harsh on my unused eyes.

I squinted them shut immediately before blinking multiple times in order to help them adjust to the blinding light. I glanced around the room before I caught sigh of a huge shadow looming behind the curtain that was pulled around my bed for privacy. My head felt fuzzy, like it was filled with cotton balls, but I strained my ears to listen in on the rest of the conversation going on.

"Alpha, there's nothing more we can do. We have done everything and exhausted every resource. I'm sorry..." Who I assumed was the pack nurse trailed off. I opened my mouth to speak, but nothing came out. It was like the Sahara Desert - so dry my vocal cords couldn't even function.

I tried once again, but only ended up coughing. I guess that would have to do. I heard two intakes of breath before the curtain was harshly ripped back, revealing my worse for wear mate. God, he looks horrible.

"A-Aceso." He cracked out, rushing to my side in seconds. He cradled my face in his hands while shaking his head back and forth like he couldn't believe I was real. "Aceso..." He rumbled out once again before tears began rolling down his face. "I thought I'd lost you!" He exclaimed, rubbing my cheeks harshly with his thumbs. I brought my hand up to rest against his own while leaning into his comforting touch. "Water?" I croaked out, barely able to speak.

"Someone get me a glass of water! NOW!" Xavier screamed to whoever was behind him. I winced at the intrusion to my ears. In seconds, the request had been filled. The room buzzed with activity, but I chose to block it all out and focus on the only two things that concerned me as of the moment: my mate, and the glass of water.

I attempted to take the glass from the nurse, but I was too weak and the glass slipped from my fingers. Xavier managed to snatch it before it smashed against the ground and brought the cup to my lips. I took long greedy gulps before closing my eyes in bliss and resting my head back against the hospital bed.

"What happened?" I finally asked after a few minutes of silence.

"After you passed out, all hell broke loose. Leighton and Charlie rushed you to the pack doctor while I ripped Jack's body to shreds. The past few months of training have been useless, being as I now have rightful ownership of Jack's pack. You slipped into a coma shortly after you got out of surgery and have been in one for the past two weeks. I kind of lost it.

"We found a cell phone on Alpha Jack's body and used it to lure his father into a trap before killing him quickly. Your father wanted to drag his death out and torture him, but I didn't want to risk him getting away and having to carry out our war plans. With that being said, I was full owner of Bloodlust and Nightshade, but I had no want or will to run their pack so I handed it over to Leighton on the condition that he sign a treaty with us as well as swearing to the Moon that he'd never let the greed for power get to him." I blinked a few times at Xavier as I processed the hoard of information he'd just thrown at me.

"I was in a coma for two weeks, Jack and his father are dead, and Leighton's Alpha of Nightshade?" I recapped, grasping the important bits of the story for my muddled brain. Then, a crippling thought made its way into my head.

"Oh my god, the baby!" I yelped, looking at him intensely.

"The baby is fine, thank the Moon." He spoke out on a relieved sigh before resting his hand upon my stomach protectively.

"No! Xavier, you don't understand. I was in this weird coma-induced place and I held our baby." I said, begging him with my eyes to believe me.

"What? How?" He questioned, suddenly much more alert than before.

"I don't know, but God, Xavier, he looks just like you." I whimpered, becoming emotional.

"He?" Xavier croaked out.

"Yes, baby, he." I affirmed. He leaned down, kissing me deeply. I pushed his chest, effectively removing his lips from mine.

"Don't. My breath is awful." I grimaced.

"I don't fucking care." He growled out before placing his lips back upon my own.

"I'm so glad you're safe. I don't know what I would've done without you." Xavier rasped out, looking pained just speaking about it.

"I love you." I replied, caressing his cheeks.

"You are my sun, moon, and stars. You are the reason I wake up every morning and the reason I want to be a better man everyday. You are my world, and I love you with everything that I am." He finished his passionate speech, sealing his words with a tender kiss.

Epilogue

Aceso's POV

One and a half years later

Stirring in bed, I hear the familiar cry of my beautiful baby boy over the monitor. I sit up in bed, realizing that I was alone. Seconds later, Xavier enters the room with our fussy toddler wriggling desperately in his grip while making dramatic grabby hands towards where I was positioned on the bed.

"Come on baby, momma will make it better!" I spoke in a high-pitched voice, taking him from Xavier's hold.

"I think that kid would like me more if I had a pair of tits." Xavier grumbled while pouting. I giggled at his words while positioning a pillow under Payton's chubby little body before beginning to nurse him. I rubbed my fingers over my little boy's head soothingly, watching as his eyes fluttered shut in content. I would have to start weaning him off of breast milk and onto real food soon, and the connection I have with him while nursing was something I was going to miss.

Xavier and I talked quietly for about twenty minutes about random pack business when I realized Payton had fallen asleep against my chest. I giggled lightly, motioning with my head for Xavier to look down.

Cradling him against my chest, I pressed my nose to his head and inhaled. His scent, a mixture of Xavier and I, was addicting. There was nothing more soothing for a she-wolf than the smell of her pups.

"Do you want me to go put him back down so you can get ready before Leighton and the lot of them arrive?" Xavier whispered. I nodded, carefully handing our son's fragile body off to him and forcing myself out of bed. Being swollen with yet another pregnancy made chasing Payton around a little difficult.

About an hour later, I wandered downstairs, hearing play-ful giggled radiating from the living room. Xavier was on all fours, playfully chasing after our son while he attempted to run away on his chubby, little baby legs. Xavier gently laid Payton on his back before pecking kisses all over his cheeks and blowing raspberries into his tummy. I smiled at the sight before me, the familiar fuzzy feeling over love blossoming in my chest.

Their play session was cut short by the doorbell.

"I got it!" I hollered before swinging the door open. Leighton's worn out form loomed in the doorway, and I shot him a sympathetic look. Charlie had just given birth to twin boys, and according to Leighton, they were absolutely re-fusing to sleep more than an hour at a time throughout the night.

"Don't worry. It'll pass." I assured him, stepping aside in order to give him enough room to slip through the door with both baby carriers in hand. Charlie followed close behind him, also looking exhausted.

"Hi, Hun. How you holding up?" I asked, pulling her tiny form in for a tight hug. She squeezed me back before replying.

"I feel like I don't do anything but breastfeed and change dirty diapers." She huffed out.

"Welcome to being a mother." I teased. "Just wait until they become mobile. It's the scariest thing ever." I stressed before turning and walking into our ridiculously baby proofed living room once again.

"Now that you're all here, I have a little news because we start setting up brunch." I said excitedly. I could tell Xavier wasn't paying attention by the stupid faces he was making at our son.

"I found out what we're having today." I said a little bit louder, trying to get Xavier's attention, but with no luck.

"And?" Charlie asked, looking more awake than she had five minutes ago.

"We're having a little girl." I replied, somewhat breathlessly.

"Oh my god!" Charlie squealed, flinging herself off the couch and onto me.

"What it! She's pregnant!" Xavier growled, finally breaking his attention away from Payton momentarily.

"I know dipshit! You're having a daughter!" Charlie goaded back. Xavier's eyes grew wide as his gaze snapped to me instantly.

"What?" He demanded, searching back and forth between my eyes with a hopeful expression.

"While you were ignoring me, I told them my exciting news. I went to the doctor yesterday and she said she could tell the sex. We're having a little girl, Xavier." I said, my voice thick with emotion. Sweeping Payton up into his arms, he rushed over to me before pulling me into a deep kiss with his unoccupied hand.

I giggled against his lips before he pulled me back in, thrusting his tongue into my mouth. Our kiss was interrupted by Payton lightly tapping on my cheek, obviously annoyed that neither of his parents were showering him with attention, like normal.

"Payton, you're gonna be a brother!" Xavier exclaimed excitedly. Though he couldn't understand Xavier's words quite yet, he bounced up and down in Xavier's arms animatedly, mimicking his father's excitement. To think I almost lost all of this years ago only makes me more thankful for everything the Moon and God has gifted me.

www.ingramcontent.com/pod-product-compliance
Lightning Source LLC
Chambersburg PA
CBHW070940190726
48292CB00004B/1267